The authors of this book have their roots in the two communities in Northern Ireland. Tom Hadden was born and bred in Portadown, a staunchly loyalist town that is a byword for hard-line attitudes even in Northern Ireland. He still lives in the townland of Derrybroughas, outside the town, where his ancestors came to live in the seventeenth century. Since 1969 he has been a lecturer in law at Queen's University, Belfast. In 1970 he was the founding editor of *Fortnight: An Independent Review for Northern Ireland*, which has established itself as the only non-partisan news magazine in Belfast and which in 1983 won the Ewart-Biggs Award for its contribution to peace and understanding in Ireland. It is read all over the world by those who really want to know what is going on in Northern Ireland. He remains a member of the editorial committee and financial director. He is also the author of *Company Law and Capitalism*.

Kevin Boyle was born and bred in Newry, an equally committed nationalist town on the border with the Republic. After qualifying as a lawyer at Queen's University, Belfast, he emerged in 1968 as a leader of the civil rights movement in Northern Ireland. From 1968 to 1977 he was a lecturer in law at Queen's University and, since 1977, has been Professor of Law at University College, Galway. As a practising barrister he has represented many of those who have taken civil rights cases to the European Commission on Human Rights. In 1984 he acted as a legal consultant to the New Ireland Forum. He is the editor of *Irish Law Texts* and an international authority on the law of human rights.

Since 1969 the authors have worked together on the operation of emergency laws in Northern Ireland. They have given evidence to numerous inquiries, from the Gardiner Committee in 1974 to the recent *Review of the Northern Ireland (Emergency Provisions) Act* by Sir George Baker. With Paddy Hillyard, they have published two major studies of the working of the law in Northern Ireland: *Law and State: The Case of Northern Ireland* (1975) and *Ten Years on in Northern Ireland* (1980). Their joint submissions to the New Ireland Forum and Northern Ireland Assembly and to the Governments in London and Dublin have been influential in recent moves towards a settlement.

Contents

Acknowledgements

The initial stimulus for this book was the request for submissions to the New Ireland Forum. The general interest in the ideas that we put to the Forum, and subsequently to the Northern Ireland Assembly's Devolution Report Committee, has encouraged us to produce this more developed and coherent statement.

We are grateful to Geraldine Cooke of Penguin Books for her enthusiasm and hard work in pressing through with the idea of a new Penguin Special on the Irish problem. We are also grateful to Dr Paul Compton of the Department of Geography at Queen's University, Belfast, for agreeing to let us use the initial results of his work on the 1981 census figures, to Rosemary Jack for her work on the various charts, to Maeve Doyle, Sub-Librarian at University College, Galway, for her assistance with notes and references, to the Controller of the Stationery Office in Dublin for permission to reproduce parts of the Forum Report, and to all those who have commented on and criticized our text and who cannot be named here. As we have had to work on the text not only from our two different perspectives but also from either side of the globe in Northern Ireland and Australia, we owe our thanks to the telex operators at Queen's University, Belfast, and La Trobe University, Melbourne, for conveying an endless stream of communications with speed and efficiency, and to the staff of the Legal Studies Department at La Trobe and to Sharon Thompson of the Faculty of Law at Queen's for coping so cheerfully and quickly with repeated corrections and amendments to the text. Our special thanks are, as always, owed to Chris Moffat and Joan Smyth for their support and encouragement and for their perceptive comments and to Mark, Rachel, Stephen, Ellen and JP for allowing us to get on with our work when we should have been doing more exciting things.

K.B.
T.H.

May 1985

Chronology of Events

1800   Act of Union creates United Kingdom of Great Britain and Ireland

1829   Catholic emancipation

1886   Gladstone's first Home Rule Bill

1893   Gladstone's second Home Rule Bill

1912   New Home Rule Bill; opposition in Ulster mobilized in Carson's Ulster Volunteer Force

1916   Easter rising in Dublin; Irish Republic proclaimed

1918   Last all-Ireland elections

1919   Declaration of Irish Republic by Sinn Féin; armed struggle for Irish independence begins

1920   Government of Ireland Act introduces partition

1921   Anglo-Irish Treaty; agreement on creation of Irish Free State and on establishment of Boundary Commission to review North–South border

1922   Civil war between pro-Treaty and anti-Treaty parties in the South

1925   Report of Boundary Commission suppressed; new Anglo-Irish Treaty confirms six-county border

1937   New Irish Constitution adopted

1948   Irish Free State becomes a Republic and leaves British Commonwealth

1949   Ireland Act affirms status of Northern Ireland as part of United Kingdom

1968   Civil rights campaign begins in Northern Ireland

1969   British troops deployed in Derry and Belfast

1971   Internment introduced

1972   Northern Ireland Parliament suspended and direct rule introduced

1973   United Kingdom and Republic join EEC; new Northern Ireland Constitution Act; elections for Northern Ireland Assembly; Sunningdale conference

1974   Power-sharing Executive established; Ulster Workers Council strike leads to collapse of Executive and dissolution of Assembly

1975   Northern Ireland Convention established

Chronology of Events

1980 Anglo-Irish Intergovernmental Council established at Thatcher/Haughey
summit
1982 Northern Ireland Assembly reconvened under Northern Ireland Act 1982
1983 New Ireland Forum established
1984 New Ireland Forum reports; Thatcher/Fitzgerald summit at Chequers

1
The Impasse: Why Everyone Despairs of the Irish Problem

Ireland is Britain's oldest problem. Britain is Ireland's. Ever since Britain became directly involved in the government of Ireland in the twelfth century there has been intermittent strife and warfare. This has traditionally been portrayed as a conflict between the British imperial state – and those it settled in Ireland – and the native Irish population. The fact that the peoples of the two islands have been inextricably mingled for thousands of years has thus been obscured. The native population of Ireland is the cumulation of successive waves of settlers from Britain and Europe. The British people is an equally complex mixture in which there has always been a very substantial Irish contribution. But this has not prevented the development of opposing national identities and cultures. The British and the Anglo-Irish are – or were – rich, Protestant and a dominant force in European and world politics. The Irish are Catholic, relatively poor and committed to neutrality. During the latter part of the nineteenth century these divergent identities became increasingly marked. The Catholic majority in Ireland, which had for so long been subjugated, began to assert itself with renewed vigour, first in the demand for religious freedom (Catholic emancipation), then in the movement for self-rule (home rule) and finally in the struggle for national independence. After a brief 'war of national liberation' the Irish problem was partially resolved in 1921–2 by a treaty between Britain and the Irish Free State that granted effective independence to most of Ireland as a dominion within the Commonwealth.

The problem was only partially resolved because, then as now, a substantial majority of the people in the six north-east counties of Ireland wanted nothing to do with either home rule or an independent Ireland and had shown themselves to be ready and able to fight against them. This local majority of Protestants had been created in the seventeenth century by the densest and most effective plantation of English and

Scottish settlers in the whole of Ireland and had maintained its distinct position during three hundred years of communal conflict with the descendants of the displaced native Catholics. It was strengthened and given a new sense of identity in 1920 by the partition of Ireland and the creation of a new constitutional entity of Northern Ireland. But this new identity was not shared by the substantial minority of nationalists whose sense of identity with the rest of Ireland was frustrated by partition. In this way the age-old Irish problem has been concentrated in a tiny part of the island. It is no less intractable. It presents, in a peculiarly stark form, opposing and equally attractive principles of self-determination and national independence. And it has generated within Northern Ireland the much less attractive practices of sectarian conflict, communal discrimination and terrorism.

For half a century the problem was left to fester. The settlement in 1921–2 freed the British political parties from fifty years of full-time preoccupation with the Irish question. Those who had been involved were more than happy to have extracted themselves by partition. Their immediate successors knew enough of the difficulties to be content to let a sleeping problem lie. In Southern Ireland the settlement of 1921–2 immediately led to a brief but bitter civil war over the 'betrayal' of the fully independent republic that had been declared in 1919. Subsequently the Irish political parties were too busy dismantling the remaining links with Britain and the Commonwealth and with building a Gaelic and Catholic state of their own to pay any real attention to Northern Ireland. They were happy to pursue the rhetoric, but not the reality, of unification. The two communities in Northern Ireland were thus left to their own devices and pursued their historic enmity with new determination. The unionists sought to protect their dominant position by creating what they hoped would be an impregnable political and economic position. The nationalist minority refused to co-operate with the new structures and continued to assert their right to be part of a unified Ireland.

In 1969 the pot boiled over. The refusal of the Unionist Party to concede the full demands of the civil rights movement and a serious outbreak of sectarian violence forced the British Government to intervene. British troops were deployed in August 1969 and soon became embroiled, as their predecessors had been through the centuries, in a seemingly endless and thankless mixture of peacekeeping and repression. The Irish Government and people were shocked into a more forceful liaison with the nationalist community in the North. The unionists retreated into ever more intransigent positions as the terrorist campaign of the Irish Republican Army (IRA) and others built up. Every initiative to improve the situation has been stubbornly and effectively resisted by one side or the other.

*In the meantime the killing and the bombing continue. To the casual observer the TV pictures and the news reports do not appear to have changed much over the past fifteen years. The scale of the death and destruction seems unimaginable in a British context. Almost 2,500 people have been killed out of a population of one and a half million. The proportional figure for Britain would be almost 100,000. Even the 'reduced' level of killing over the past few years, at around 100 a year, would work out at between 3,000 and 4,000 a year for Britain. The proportional figures for damage to property are almost as striking. The total of more than £1,000 million paid out in official compensation over the years would be equivalent to almost £40 billion for the whole of Britain. And that pales into insignificance if the total cost to Britain of its commitment in Northern Ireland, both in maintaining British standards in social security and other spheres and in security costs – currently almost £1,500 million *per year* – is included. The direct and indirect cost to the Republic of extra security and lost revenue from tourism – estimated by the New Ireland Forum at some £2,000 million between 1969 and 1982 – has been proportionally three or four times as large (see Tables 1 and 2).[1]

How can people in Northern Ireland – the reasonable Briton may ask – go on living in such a terrible environment? How can parents bring up their children there? Why can they not agree to some reasonable compromise? And if they cannot, why should Britain go on and on paying such a high price in cash and in the lives of its young soldiers for no benefit at all? Why should Britain not withdraw its troops and its subsidy immediately or at any rate after giving due notice to allow something to be agreed by the Irish themselves? And in any case what is so wrong with unification – the policy of the Labour Party and the first choice of the New Ireland Forum – or with the alternatives of an all-Ireland federation or even of joint authority between Britain and Ireland, as suggested by the Forum and recommended by the British Kilbrandon Committee? What could be worse than just soldiering on with policies that have been achieving so little for so long?

The first batch of these questions is quite easy to answer. For most of the people in Northern Ireland the TV pictures and the news reports of killings and bombings and riots are almost as distant in psychological terms as they are for people in Britain. Almost everyone in Northern Ireland goes about his or her business in exactly the same way as people in Britain and the rest of Ireland. In purely statistical terms

Table 1

The impact of the 'troubles'

The impact of the 'troubles' should be measured in communal as well as absolute terms; this table shows that in the initial years many more Catholics than Protestants were killed, but that since 1976 the death toll in the Protestant community, among both civilians and members of local security forces, has been higher.

Year	Total incidents	Total deaths	Catholics		Protestants		Security forces		Other
			Civilian	IRA, etc.	Civilian	UVF,* etc.	Local	British	
1969	n/a	15	7	1	6	—	1	—	—
1970	368	25	8	5	8	—	2	—	2
1971	2,789	173	62	17	31	—	16	43	4
1972	12,123	474	166	65	74	10	42	107	10
1973	6,025	252	75	32	50	8	21	58	8
1974	3,875	221	95	17	50	4	24	27	4
1975	2,169	244	104	17	69	18	18	13	5
1976	2,571	296	124	14	95	5	40	14	4
1977	1,447	114	33	6	19	6	30	16	4
1978	1,210	70	9	7	21	—	19	12	2
1979	1,150	106	17	5	14	—	30	38	2
1980	922	78	20	4	19	1	19	12	3
1981	1,213	108	27	16	15	3	33	11	3
1982	601	95	20	9	18	4	21	20	3
1983	556	77	44				28	5	—
1984	423	64	36				19	9	—

* Ulster Volunteer Force.

Notes: Incidents include shootings and bombings recorded by the Royal Ulster Constabulary; the figures for deaths are taken from the analysis by the New Ireland Forum, updated to 1984; prison officers are listed as 'local security forces', almost all of whom were Protestant; 'other' includes civilians not resident in Northern Ireland and other unclassified deaths.

Table 2

The cost of the 'troubles' and of the British subvention

The financial cost of the 'troubles' falls on both Britain and Ireland. Though the cost of compensation for death and damage to property has stabilized, the extra cost of British Army operations and of non-security support for Northern Ireland continues to rise. The extra cost to the Republic of security alone is as large per head of its population as total British support for Northern Ireland. The contribution to Northern Ireland from the European Community is still minimal.

Year	Compensation for death and property loss (£m)	Extra cost of British Army (£m)	Total British support for NI (£m)	(£ per head)	Extra cost to Republic of security (IR£m)	(IR£ per head)	European support for NI (£m)
1968/69	—	—	74	1	—	—	—
1969/70	2	1	75	1	2	1	—
1970/71	3	6	94	2	3	1	—
1971/72	5	14	140	3	7	2	—
1972/73	29	29	209	4	11	4	—
1973/74	32	33	351	6	15	5	—
1974/75	46	45	464	8	15	5	3
1975/76	54	60	656	12	33	10	3
1976/77	56	65	707	13	40	12	13
1977/78	45	69	769	14	47	14	14
1978/79	50	81	979	18	55	17	19
1979/80	48	96	1,086	20	60	18	31
1980/81	55	111	1,248	23	79	24	44
1981/82	43	149	1,259	23	98	29	41
1982/83	n/a	143	1,365	25	125	36	53
1983/84	n/a	141	1,507	28	136	39	67
1984/85	n/a	121	1,671	30	147	42	69

Notes: The figures for security costs are taken from the New Ireland Forum study *The Cost of Violence Arising from the Northern Ireland Crisis since 1969*; those for British and European support are taken from the New Ireland Forum study *A Comparative Description of the Economic Structure and Situation, North and South*, Appendix 4, Table 14. From 1974 the figures for security costs in the Republic are for calendar years. The figures for 1983/84 and 1984/85 have been added. EEC support for Northern Ireland is paid direct to the British Treasury and might therefore be deducted from the figure for total British support; payments under the Common Agricultural Policy are not included.

the risk of being caught up in terrorist or sectarian violence is really quite low. The risk of death or serious injury as a result of the 'troubles' is now less than half the risk of being killed or injured in a traffic accident (see Figure 1).[2] It is far more dangerous to live in New York or Detroit or many other large American cities than it is to live in Belfast. This may not seem much comfort to people in Britain and the Irish Republic. They might be more impressed by the fact that it is more dangerous for someone to take a holiday in France, where the figures for road deaths are now double those in Northern Ireland, than to take a holiday in Ulster. The point of these facts is not that more tourists should be encouraged to come to Ulster. It is that for most people in Northern Ireland the troubles are less significant in practical terms than the ordinary risks of twentieth-century living. There is communal outrage and anger over particularly terrible incidents. But people have learned to cope with the level of violence and disruption that they have become used to, just as people in the USA, Britain and France can cope perfectly well with their respective levels of violence and accidental death and injury. The same may be said about the economic effects of the 'troubles'. For most people the impact of the 'troubles' in financial terms is much less than the impact of the recession

 Figure 1

The risk of death in Northern Ireland and other countries

The risk of being killed in Northern Ireland as a result of the 'troubles' has long been much less than the risk of being killed on the roads. The combined risk of being killed in the 'troubles' and on the roads is now much less than the combined risk of being murdered or killed on the roads in France and the United States.

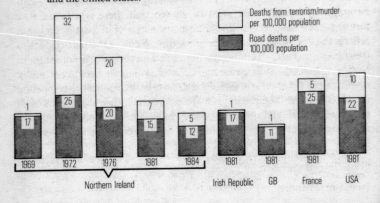

16

throughout the world. The general level of unemployment has always been a little worse than in the worst areas of Britain, but not much worse.

There are, of course, exceptions. The risk of death or injury among members of the security forces and paramilitary organizations on either side is very much higher. The levels of unemployment among the minority community have long been more than double those in the majority community and are worse than anywhere in Britain. The general quality of life in the most troubled areas, which are concentrated in Catholic areas in Belfast, Derry,* Newry and other towns is anything but pleasant. It is precisely this combination – complacency and relative prosperity in the majority community, fear and antagonism among members of the security forces and a high degree of general disaffection among large sections of the minority community – that makes it likely that the violence and instability will continue indefinitely, or at least until some more radical policies than have yet been tried are successfully implemented.

Providing answers to the second batch of questions will be more difficult. The starting point must be an explanation of why it is that the various parties to the conflict so resolutely refuse to be reasonable. When that aspect of the problem is better understood, it may be easier to persuade those who are concerned about the issues, but have begun to realize that there is more to them than they first thought, that any realistic settlement must be more complex. But that will not be enough for those who already know they know the right answer to the Irish problem. They must first be convinced that none of the radical and seemingly straightforward solutions that have been canvassed in recent years – from unification or federation for Ireland as a whole to independence for Northern Ireland or just a unilateral British withdrawal – can be made to work. Then it must be shown that there is a better way forward – one that recognizes the responsibilities of all parties and that reflects the complexity of their relationships. None of the participants in the present impasse – Britain, the Republic and the two communities in Northern Ireland – has clean hands. And none can avoid continuing involvement. Any realistic settlement must take account of the competing senses of history, the present grievances and the future aspirations of all of those involved and must adequately reflect the interlocking relationships between the two communities in Northern Ireland, between

*In accordance with our proposed principle that the majority of the population in a given area should be entitled to determine its name we have called the city Derry and the county Londonderry to reflect their respective Catholic and Protestant majorities.

The Impasse

Northern Ireland and the Republic and between Britain and Ireland. This cannot be done within the rigid and outmoded concepts of national independence and separation. New and more flexible models are required. That is what this book is about.

2
The Simple Solutions: Why They will not Work

One of the most striking things about the Irish problem is that there are so many solutions. Literally hundreds of possible settlements have been proposed. More books have been published on Northern Ireland than can be listed, let alone discussed, here.[1] But there is no difficulty in identifying the most obvious and seemingly straightforward solutions. The most popular is, of course, unification, which the New Ireland Forum and the British Labour Party wish to achieve by consent and which the Provisional IRA and its political counterpart, Provisional Sinn Féin, wish to attain by force. All these seem also prepared to contemplate some form of federal Ireland in which Northern Ireland or Ulster would be able to maintain a separate identity. At the other extreme are the ideas of an independent Northern Ireland or the total integration of the six northern counties with the rest of Britain. In between there is a huge range of variations, from indefinite maintenance of the current structures for direct rule from London to more elaborate arrangements for sharing control between London and Dublin. There is also the possibility of redrawing the boundary between Northern Ireland and the rest of Ireland.

Another striking thing about all these solutions is that none of them has been successfully implemented and that many have never even been tried. Is this because they have not been pursued with sufficient determination? Or is it because they are not workable?

The answer for all the most radical and apparently straightforward solutions is, regrettably, that they cannot be expected to work. That is not to say that they are not sensible or desirable. The problem is that they cannot be put into operation in the real world. Too many of those who favour such solutions pay no attention at all to how they are to be achieved – unification by consent is the best example – or to what is likely to happen if they are imposed, as with a unilateral British withdrawal. Determination alone is not sufficient to resolve the Irish problem.

Realism about the determination and strength of those who oppose what appear to others to be simple solutions is also required.

① Unification – the Republican Ideal and the New Ireland Forum

The idea of Ireland as a natural political unit that must ultimately be united in a single independent state is deeply embedded in the nationalist and republican traditions. There is little historical foundation for the idea.[2] Ireland has never been united in a single independent state. The northern part of the island was for centuries more closely linked with Scotland, both in its population and in its political structures, than with the rest of Ireland. It was the British conquest that first unified Ireland in any real sense. But commitment to the ideal of unification is deeply rooted in the Republic, in the nationalist community in Northern Ireland and among Irish emigrants throughout the world. The only significant dispute has been whether the ideal can be achieved only by force, as is argued by the IRA and its supporters, or whether it can be achieved peacefully and by consent, as argued by the British Labour Party in its new Irish policy document adopted in 1981 and by the New Ireland Forum Report in 1984.

Until the establishment of the New Ireland Forum in 1983 supporters of the 'armed struggle' could certainly claim to be the only serious proponents of the republican ideal. As will be seen below, the commitment to unification on the part of successive Irish Governments since 1920 was almost exclusively rhetorical. No opportunity was missed by the leaders of the newly independent state to assert its exclusively Catholic, Gaelic and non-British ethos and, in so doing, to confirm the fears and prejudices of northern Protestants and to deter them from contemplating any form of unity or even mutual respect. These policies and the regular assertion of the ultimate objective of incorporating the whole of Ireland within the Republic without taking any account of the views and interests of northern Protestants merely served to strengthen their determination to have nothing to do with the Republic. The unionists, for their part, sought to create an exclusively British ethos in Northern Ireland and to deny the Irish identity of northern Catholics. To this extent traditional Irish nationalism and Ulster unionism were mutually self-supporting. The eventual realization by nationalists of the impracticality of achieving unification by consent without making more explicit the way in which the identity and interests of northern Protestants would be protected was the principal reason for the setting up of the New Ireland Forum.

The more immediate cause of the setting up of the Forum was the fear among nationalists who rejected violence that if nothing was done, Provisional Sinn Féin would be likely to outvote the Social Democratic and Labour Party (SDLP), the established party of the Catholic people of Northern Ireland, in the European elections of June 1984. John Hume, the leader of the SDLP, persuaded the leaders of the three main parties in the Republic – Fianna Fáil, Fine Gael and the Irish Labour Party – that a new effort by constitutional nationalists to reach agreement on how unification might be achieved was essential if the situation in Northern Ireland were not to deteriorate further. The New Ireland Forum was therefore established in the summer of 1983 with the express purpose of finding a way in which 'lasting peace and stability could be achieved in a New Ireland through the democratic process'.

It was originally hoped that the report of the Forum would be ready in a few months. But the volume of evidence submitted to it and the difficulty in securing agreement between the delegates of the four constituent parties resulted in successive postponements. The pressure on all those involved to produce a report in time to influence the results of the European election and the feeling that nothing less than a unanimous report would be worth while gave Charles Haughey, leader of the traditionally republican Fianna Fáil, a golden opportunity to make it a condition of his agreement that simple unification, with appropriate protections for northern Protestants, would be endorsed. The final report of the Forum in May 1984 thus stated that 'a united Ireland in the form of a sovereign independent Irish state to be achieved peacefully and by consent' was 'the best and most durable basis for peace and stability' (paras. 5.4 and 5.5) and that a unitary state 'would embrace the whole island of Ireland governed as a single unit under one government and one parliament elected by all the people of the island' (para. 6.1).[3] It is questionable whether this was the true objective of the other participants, who appear to have favoured, as more realistic and attainable, the alternative options of a federal state or a system of joint authority under which both London and Dublin would have equal responsibility for the government of Northern Ireland. Following the publication of the Forum Report the participants diverged sharply on how it should be interpreted. Charles Haughey insisted that it endorsed immediate action to bring about a unitary state. Garret Fitzgerald and Dick Spring, leaders of the governing Fine Gael/Irish Labour Party coalition, and John Hume repeatedly stressed the open-ended nature of the report and laid emphasis

21

more on the list of 'realities and requirements' – notably the need to accommodate both traditions – that were identified as essential to any lasting settlement than on any single option (see Appendix). But it was the apparent endorsement of the traditional nationalist ideal of simple unification that made the most immediate impact. If any of the other options are to be treated seriously, the impracticality of simple unification, whether by force or by consent, must be conclusively demonstrated.

Was Partition Avoidable?

One of the principal arguments of those who support unification is that partition was imposed by Britain against the will of the Irish people. The Forum Report emphasizes the fact that in the last all-Ireland election of 1918 a clear majority of the Irish people voted for independence for the whole of Ireland and reiterates the traditional nationalist claim that 'the intention underlying the creation of Northern Ireland was to establish a political unit containing the largest land area that was consistent with maintaining a permanent majority of unionists' (paras. 3.1 and 3.2). The British Government is thus in effect blamed for creating the problem through the terms of the 1920 partition settlement. The British response is that partition was unavoidable. What were the facts?

The idea of partition was first seriously raised in 1912, when it became clear that very large numbers of Protestants in Ulster who had joined Sir Edward Carson's Ulster Volunteer Force (UVF) were prepared to fight against the imposition of home rule by Britain on an all-Ireland basis. There was heated argument at the time about whether all nine counties in Ulster should be excluded or whether a four- or six-county unit would make more sense. The choice of the six-county unit appears to have been made on pragmatic grounds, as the most readily identifiable area in which most of the unionists lived. Figure 2(i) shows the population figures on which the decision was made. It was eventually agreed in the Anglo-Irish Treaty of 1921 that the line of the border should be reviewed by a Boundary Commission in the light of the wishes of local inhabitants. But the unionists boycotted the Commission, and its report in 1925 (which was leaked but never formally published) recommended changes that were too marginal to be acceptable to nationalists (see Figure 2(ii)).[4]

The idea that the rest of Ireland had to be granted a measure of independence rather than merely home rule within the United Kingdom was similarly accepted when it became clear after the election of 1918 that the vast majority of voters in the twenty-six counties supported the objectives of Sinn Féin and that the guerrilla campaign by the IRA could not be contained. It is true that the British Government made no attempt to coerce the unionists and that it did its best to suppress the IRA. It is also true that the adoption of partition as a solution, however temporary, may be linked to other contemporary British concerns, both political and military, and that the way in which the Boundary Commission set about its work added to nationalist suspicions of British motives. The underlying reason for the partition of Ireland was none the less that the vast majority of the people in the six counties and the twenty-six counties respectively had expressed wholly incompatible loyalties and commitments and had shown themselves to be willing and able to fight for those loyalties and commitments. The truth, in crude terms, is that both the Republic and Northern Ireland were created by a combination of military force and popular will.

Why Partition Remains

Very little has changed in the years since 1920, either in the balance of population within Northern Ireland or in terms of the ability of unionists to resist unification.

To begin with it is clear from the results of the 1981 census in Northern Ireland not only that the increase in the proportion of Catholics

Table 3

Communal population changes in Northern Ireland, 1971–81

Recent census figures indicate that the higher birth rate among Catholics in Northern Ireland is largely offset by a higher emigration rate and that the increase in the proportion of Catholics has been very small.

	Protestants and others		Catholics	
1971 estimate	965,000	63.2%	562,000	36.8%
natural increase	30,000		78,000	
net emigration	53,500		76,500	
1981 estimate	941,000	62.5%	563,000	37.5%

Source: *Fortnight*, issue 192, March 1983; a later estimate by Dr Compton suggests a figure for Catholics in 1981 of between 37.6 and 38.6 per cent. An estimate made for the Fair Employment Agency suggests a figure of 39.1 per cent (D. Eversley and V. Herr, *The Roman Catholic Population of Northern Ireland in 1981*, 1985).

in Northern Ireland since the 1920s has been relatively small, despite the continuing higher birth rate among Catholics, but also that it would be unrealistic to predict any rapid change in the foreseeable future. The detailed work on the demography of the two communities carried out by Dr Paul Compton at Queen's University, Belfast, shows that a higher emigration rate among Catholics has continued to counterbalance higher Catholic fertility. His initial estimates indicate that, as in earlier decades, the net inter-censal emigration between 1971 and 1981 was about 14 per cent for Catholics compared with about 6 per cent for Protestants and that the Catholic proportion of the population in 1981 was some 37.5 per cent compared with a figure of some 33.5 per cent in 1926, as shown in Table 3. Compton concludes that if Catholic fertility and family size continue to fall during the 1980s, as he predicts, 'there can

Figure 2

The Basis of Partition

Once partition had been decided on, where should the border have been drawn? These maps show (i) the Catholic population of the nine counties of Ulster and of Belfast and Derry as a proportion of the total population in 1901, and (ii) the draft recommendations of the abortive Boundary Commission in 1925.

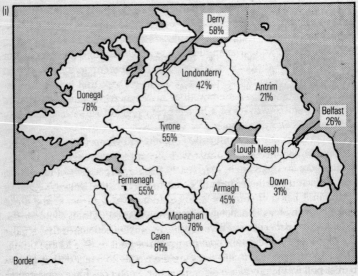

24

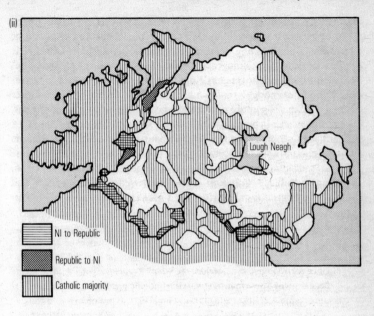

(ii)

Lough Neagh

NI to Republic

Republic to NI

Catholic majority

be no automatic assumption that present trends will remain unchanged and that Catholics will eventually become the majority community in the province.'[5] Even if these figures underestimate the current proportion of Catholics, as argued at the Forum hearings, no one doubts that for the foreseeable future there will be a clear Protestant majority in Northern Ireland.[6] The more significant conclusion is perhaps that in any foreseeable circumstances *both* communities in Northern Ireland are going to be of sufficient size to make it impractical to regard either as a minority that can effectively be ignored.

It is equally clear that the commitment of northern Protestants to the maintenance of the union with Britain is unchanged. In the last official vote on the issue in March 1973 some 58 per cent of the voting population in Northern Ireland voted to stay in the United Kingdom; less than 1 per cent voted for a united Ireland; and 41 per cent did not vote. Allowing for the deliberate abstention of most Catholics and for the usual 20–25 per cent of non-voters, it can only be concluded that almost the whole of the Protestant community turned out to vote for the union. There is no evidence from recent opinion polls to suggest that a new border poll would produce a different result. Such polls have consistently reported that a substantial number of Catholics would be content to remain within the United Kingdom and that virtually no Protestants would be content to join a united Ireland. For example, in the Northern Ireland Attitude Survey carried out in 1978 only 4 per cent of Protestants favoured any form of united Ireland, while about half the Catholics supported various forms of settlement within the United Kingdom; and in a MORI Poll carried out in 1984, 86 per cent of Protestants were strongly opposed to granting any say to the Republic over constitutional changes in Northern Ireland, while 50 per cent of Catholics were prepared to accept a devolved system of government for Northern Ireland within the United Kingdom, with special guarantees for Catholics.

Nor can the commitment and the ability of many members of the Protestant community to use force to maintain their position be seriously doubted. The current strength of the Ulster Defence Regiment (UDR), which is drawn almost exclusively from the Protestant community and which was formed for the express purpose of the defence of Northern Ireland, is some 7,500. The current strength of the Royal Ulster Constabulary (RUC) is 8,000 and of the RUC Reserve some 4,500, and despite efforts to recruit them the proportion of Catholics is less than 10 per cent, not least because Catholic members of the police are frequently singled out for assassination by the IRA. All these forces are well-armed, and though they are officially non-sectarian, there can be little doubt that the majority of those in them would resist any attempt by Britain to impose unification. Moreover, if such a policy were adopted, it is almost certain that many more members of the Protestant community would be ready to join official or unofficial paramilitary organizations, as they did in the early 1920s and again on the imposition of direct rule in 1972, and that if it were not possible to defend the union, the defence of an independent Northern Ireland would be adopted as an alternative. It seems equally certain that in the absence of external intervention the Protestant community in Northern Ireland would prevail over the Catholic community in any serious armed conflict.

It should be added that this commitment on the part of northern Protestants to maintain the union and to resist absorption in a united Ireland is not directly linked to the maintenance of a majority within the six counties. Even if there were to be a substantial change in the voting power of the two communities and a majority were to vote for unification, it would be unwise to expect a peaceful resolution of the conflict on that ground alone. On the contrary, it is more likely that communal tensions and the risk of violence would increase rather than decrease as the balance of voting power became more equal.

Legitimacy and Consent

These facts have a direct bearing on the legitimacy of partition and thus of Northern Ireland. It is a fundamental tenet of Irish nationalists that Northern Ireland is not a legitimate state. They argue that the vote of the majority of the Irish people for Sinn Féin in 1918 gave a clear mandate for unity and independence and that neither the British Government nor the northern unionists had any right to frustrate their achievement. If unification had been denied only by the British Government and if partition had been adopted against the wishes both of the nationalist majority in Ireland and of the unionist majority in Northern Ireland, that argument would be tenable in international law. But that was not what happened. On the contrary, legitimacy can properly be claimed for the current constitutional status of Northern Ireland on two internationally recognized grounds: first, in that a substantial majority of its citizens have consistently expressed their support, in free and fair elections, for union with Britain; and, secondly, in that in the event of an armed conflict within its boundaries it is almost certain that the unionist community would be able to maintain an effective system of government. The first of these is the universally accepted principle of self-determination. The second is tacitly accepted in the international community in that the victors of an internal conflict or of a revolutionary *coup d'état* are entitled to be granted first *de facto* and ultimately *de jure* recognition.

It must be conceded that on a broader concept of legitimacy that requires the general acceptance of a state by substantially all of its citizens Northern Ireland is not a legitimate political entity. Nor would a united Ireland have been in 1920. Nor would it be now. It must also be conceded that those responsible for the government of Northern Ireland have failed to meet the highest internationally accepted standards in the treatment of its communal minority and in matters of internal security. The same might be said of many other states whose legitimacy is not questioned. The more usual response to such criticisms is to demand that the treatment of the minority be improved. Finally it must be conceded that the border between Northern Ireland and the Republic could have been drawn in a more satisfactory way. But there was no wholly satisfactory boundary.

None of these points detracts from the right of Britain in the 1920s to recognize by partition the conflicting wishes of a substantial majority of the people in two well-defined parts of Ireland. Nor can there be any question as to Britain's continuing right to maintain partition in defence of the right of a majority in Northern Ireland to self-determination. What can be questioned and criticized is Britain's total failure to balance its concern for the rights of the unionist majority with equal concern for those of the nationalist minority locked into a state of which they wanted no part. The abandonment of control over part of the United Kingdom to a local majority with minimal safeguards for the minority and the failure over more than fifty years to correct the ensuing abuses together justify a grave indictment of British policy in a province for which Britain has always borne the ultimate responsibility.

The fundamental point in this analysis – that no change in the status of Northern Ireland can be democratically made until the majority of its people desire it – has been accepted by successive Irish Governments since the joint Sunningdale declaration in 1973. It was also tacitly accepted in the Forum Report, which firmly rejected 'attempts from any quarter to impose a particular solution through violence' and asserted with equal clarity that 'the political arrangements for a new and sovereign Ireland would have to be freely negotiated and agreed to by the people of the North and by the people of the South' (para. 5.2). But, having enunciated the principle of consent, the Forum Report proceeds to ignore its implications in adopting a unitary state as its preferred option and in calling on the British Government to take immediate action to resolve the Northern Ireland crisis. For if the principle of consent, and the corresponding right of unionists to say no to a united Ireland, are treated seriously, much of the discussion in the Forum Report is of academic rather than practical concern, since it is clear to all that the consent of unionists to any of the options proposed is not forthcoming. If the Forum had unambiguously adopted unification as an aspiration that could be realized only with the consent of unionists, its report would have made a more constructive contribution. A brief account of the form of unification proposed by the Forum and of its alternative options of federation or joint authority must none the less be given, if only to clarify the implications of their summary rejection by Mrs Thatcher in her notorious 'Out, out, out' speech after the Anglo-Irish summit in November 1984.

The Forum Options

A Unitary State

If the fundamental political objection to unification on the part of unionists could be overcome, the model of a unitary state proposed in the Forum Report would not be unreasonable. It is suggested that northern Protestants might be guaranteed a minimum level of representation in a Senate with blocking powers on issues of major communal importance; that weighted voting majorities might be required for any legislation on certain prescribed matters; that individual and communal rights would be guaranteed, notably in respect of the two main educational systems and the two main cultural traditions; that those who wished to retain their British identity would be entitled to dual British and Irish citizenship; and that new institutions would be established to reflect the unique relationship between Britain and Ireland. As will be seen, many of these ideas might appropriately be applied in reverse to the protection of the rights and interests of Irish nationalists within Northern Ireland and the United Kingdom.

There are some other, more practical, objections to unification that contribute to the reluctance of unionists even to consider it. The most significant is financial. The Forum Report stresses the economic benefits of unification in terms of integrated industrial and agricultural policies. But it does not provide a convincing answer to the replacement of the very substantial subvention from the British Treasury that Northern Ireland is currently entitled to as a depressed region within the United Kingdom. A study commissioned by the Forum of the economic implications of unification demonstrates that it would be virtually impossible in present circumstances for the Republic to provide an equivalent subvention and concludes that if Northern Ireland alone were to bear the cost, the resulting financial imbalances 'would be so severe that the adjustment in living standards would be unconscionable'.[7] The only possible conclusion to be drawn from this analysis is that a substantial British subvention over an extended period would be necessary if unification were to be economically viable. Unionists are clearly entitled to ask why they should willingly give up a subvention that, like other depressed regions in the United Kingdom, they receive as of right in return for a much less certain economic future in a united Ireland.

A Federal or Confederal State

The idea of a federal Ireland has frequently been proposed as a means of achieving a united and independent Ireland without depriving northern Protestants of some degree of self-government. This might help to resolve some of the differences on matters of social legislation between the predominantly Protestant community in the North and the almost exclusively Catholic community in the rest of Ireland. It may also be argued that since under the 1920 settlement the unionists never enjoyed more than the limited powers of a subordinate Parliament in a state in which authority on such matters as defence, foreign relations and taxation has been reserved for central government, their effective power in a federal Ireland would be no less. In its discussion of this option the Forum Report draws a distinction between a federal constitution, in which residual power on matters not explicitly conferred on the constituent states is conferred on the central or federal Government, and a confederal constitution, in which the central or confederal Government may exercise only powers expressly conferred on it by the constituent states. Though the distinction is largely formal, there may be some political advantage in the confederal model, in that the representatives both of the Republic and of Northern Ireland would be seen to be ceding certain explicit powers to a newly established joint confederation rather than submerging their established identities in a federal state.

The principal difficulties with either of these models, as with simple unification, are those of obtaining the consent of unionists and making satisfactory arrangements to replace the British subvention. But there are other more specific problems. Federal systems of government depend on a basic level of agreement as to national objectives that could not be assumed to exist in the case of the Republic and Northern Ireland. There is a deeply felt commitment to independence and neutrality within the Republic, most recently expressed over the Falklands war, which is not shared by unionists. There would also be a fundamental imbalance in the constituent parts of an Irish federation unless a new set of provincial governments were established within the Republic. The corresponding imbalance between the populations of England, Wales, Scotland and Northern Ireland has proved to be a major obstacle to the idea of a federal United Kingdom, given the lack of any real desire for regional government within England. Nor is it clear how the interests of the nationalist minority within a federal Northern Ireland would be protected. This poses a difficult dilemma for proponents of an Irish federation: the larger the powers of the central federal Government, the less likely it is – though it is in any event highly unlikely – that unionists would agree to it; but if the powers of the central federal Government were severely restricted, the more necessary it would be to provide effective protections for the minority within Northern Ireland, thus raising the very problems that have proved so intractable within the existing constitutional framework.

Joint Authority

The third option considered by the Forum is a system of joint authority under which 'the London and Dublin Governments would have equal responsibility for all aspects of the government of Northern Ireland' so as to accord equal validity to the two traditions in Northern Ireland and reflect the reality of their divided allegiances (para. 8.1). The phrase 'joint authority' appears to have been chosen in preference to 'joint sovereignty' to permit Britain to grant some direct responsibility for the government of Northern Ireland to the Republic without breaking its repeated guarantee that Northern Ireland would not cease to be part of the United Kingdom without the consent of the majority of voters in Northern Ireland.

The mechanisms for the exercise of joint authority are not explored in any detail. What appears to be envisaged is a more or less permanent system of direct rule with a number of Ministers representing both London and Dublin. Nor are the proposed arrangements for finance explained. The Report merely states that 'the overall level of public expenditure would be determined by the two Governments' (para. 8.6). The economic study commissioned by the Forum, while it is not expressly adopted, however, suggests that tax in Northern Ireland might continue to be levied at British rates and that the cost of subvention would be borne jointly by Britain and the Republic in proportion to their respective gross national products.[8]

This method of accommodating the competing claims of Britain and the Republic over Northern Ireland is initially attractive. It would recognize the fact that both states have an interest in Northern Ireland that neither can afford to be seen to abandon, however much it may be suspected that both would like to be able to do so. It would give both communities in Northern Ireland a means of asserting their citizenship of the state to which they wish to belong. It might help to resolve some of the persistent security problems that arise from the existence of two entirely separate legal jurisdictions north and south of the border. And it might prove to be to Northern Ireland's advantage in its dealings with the European Community. But there are equally substantial drawbacks to joint authority of the kind proposed by the Forum. The most important is the strong opposition among unionists to any form of direct control by the Republic over the affairs of Northern Ireland. There is no discussion at all in the Forum Report as to how the co-operation of unionists might be encouraged. Nor is there any discussion of how the authority of the two sovereign states is to be exercised, notably in respect of legislation for Northern Ireland, or of how differences on what should be done are to be resolved. There is also a problem over the democratic involvement of the people of Northern Ireland. The precedents for joint authority in the Sudan and the New Hebrides involved the division of the spoils of conquest by two colonial powers without reference to the wishes of the local inhabitants. Though there is a brief reference in the Forum Report to the possibility of the devolution of some powers to a local assembly, the form that this might take and the way in which the people of Northern Ireland would be represented, if at all, in the Parliaments at Westminster and Dublin are not explained. Though some of the ideas in this part of the Report might be acceptable in an alternative context, as will be seen, the joint-authority model as proposed by the Forum cannot form the basis of settlement.

An Independent Northern Ireland

The ideas of unification, federation and the form of joint authority proposed by the New Ireland Forum approach the Northern Ireland problem from an essentially nationalist point of view in that they are designed to extend the authority of the Irish Republic, in one form or another, over the whole island of Ireland. The most radical of the solutions proposed from an essentially unionist point of view is that Northern Ireland should be established as an independent state within the European Community but free of any subordination to either Britain or the Republic.

The underlying argument of those like the New Ulster Political Research Group, an offshoot of the loyalist paramilitary Ulster Defence Association, who support an independent Northern Ireland is that the people of Northern Ireland are, and have always been, distinct and different from those in the rest of Ireland, and that if the conflicting loyalties to both Britain and the Republic were removed, both communities would be better able to realize their common interests and identity. They also argue that the obvious problem over the financial viability of an independent Northern Ireland could be overcome by a combination of continuing aid from Britain, which might gradually be replaced by aid from the European Commission, and a much heavier reliance on direct government borrowing than has been permitted to the Northern Ireland Department of Finance as a subordinate unit within the United Kingdom. A number of established economists have stated that this is not an entirely unrealistic proposal, provided that an independent Northern Ireland could create a peaceful and stable environment for economic development.[9] It has been suggested that this might be achieved by a political system of checks and balances modelled on the American constitution – with an elected President and Vice-President from the two communities – and an entrenched Bill of Rights to protect individual and communal rights.

The major objection to an independent Northern Ireland is that this kind of stability cannot be predicted with any certainty. The independence option has never gained more than a tiny proportion of first-preference votes in any opinion poll and has been found to be acceptable to many more Protestants than Catholics. It seems likely that independence would be adopted by many unionists as a last resort in the face of a threatened or actual British withdrawal, as the only means of avoiding some form of unification with the Republic. It seems unlikely that it would prove acceptable to most nationalists, who might reasonably fear that it would amount to little more than a return to simple majority rule on the old Stormont model without even the protection of possible British intervention against discriminatory treatment. It also seems likely that it would be regarded by the IRA and other nationalist paramilitary bodies merely as the successful achievement of their initial goal of expelling the British from Ireland through their sustained campaign of violence and thus as further proof that continuance of that campaign is the only means of securing the ultimate goal of unification. The resulting need for stringent security measures on the part of a predominantly Protestant Government in Catholic areas would then be likely to destroy any chance that the bulk of the Catholic community would throw their weight behind the new arrangements. Even if the initial consent of the majority of both communities could be achieved, which is doubtful, an independent Northern Ireland might thus degenerate into civil strife and warfare.

Integration

Another solution that would meet the wishes of unionists would be the full integration of Northern Ireland with the rest of the United Kingdom. This would involve abandoning the attempt to find an acceptable form for devolved government in Northern Ireland and reinstating a standard British form of local government. Though in administrative and legislative terms there has already been a good deal of creeping integration under direct rule, the British Government has consistently made it clear that full and open integration is not on offer. At the Sunningdale conference in 1973 it made a formal declaration that it would 'support' the unification of Ireland if the people of Northern Ireland wished it. Since then it has repeatedly stressed that direct rule is a temporary expedient pending the devolution of powers on an agreed basis. And on a more down-to-earth level it has refused to integrate Northern Ireland in any new governmental arrangements for Britain, notably in respect of the exclusion of the Belfast shipbuilders, Harland and Wolff, from the nationalized British Shipbuilders. It seems likely that this policy stems from a pragmatic determination by successive British Governments not to become permanently involved in the quagmire of Ulster politics. The more fundamental objection to integration is that it assumes that Northern Ireland is wholly British in identity, whereas in reality it shares both British and Irish identities. Integration is for that reason completely unacceptable to the nationalist community in Northern Ireland. If the policy of unification must be rejected because it ignores the reality of the unionist veto, the policy of integration must also be rejected because it ignores the reality of the nationalist veto.

(7) Repartition

An alternative method of meeting the wishes of unionists for the continuance of a separate Northern Ireland state, whether within the United Kingdom or as an independent member of the European Community, would be to redraw the boundary between Northern Ireland and the Republic. The object of this would be to follow the logic of partition by creating two states in Ireland, one of which would be almost exclusively Protestant and the other almost exclusively Catholic, and thus to avoid the problems caused by the divergent loyalties and aspirations of the two communities in Northern Ireland.

This is an initially attractive proposition. But there would be very substantial practical difficulties in putting it into effect. The distribution of the two communities in Northern Ireland in the 1980s, as in the 1920s, is not such that any border can be drawn that would not leave a significant and potentially disaffected minority on the wrong side. Figure 3(i) shows clearly that in general terms the proportion of Protestants is highest in the area around Belfast and that it declines gradually towards the border. In the thirteen districts around Belfast that constitute the Protestant 'heartland' the proportion of Protestants in 1981 ranged from 62 per cent in Belfast itself to over 90 per cent in North Down, Castlereagh and Carrickfergus. In the adjacent districts of Moyle, Limavady, Maghera-felt, Cookstown, Dungannon, Armagh and Craigavon it ranged from 59 to 43 per cent. And in the remaining border districts of Derry, Strabane, Omagh, Fermanagh, Newry and Mourne, and Down it ranged from 46 to only 26 per cent. The position is further complicated by the fact that the progression towards a Catholic majority in border areas is not even. There are pockets of high Catholic density miles away from the border, as in the districts of Moyle and Magherafelt. The largest concentration of Catholics

– more than 150,000 in all – is in Greater Belfast. There are also areas where there is a small majority of Protestants, or rough equality, on or near the border, as in the river valleys to the south and west of counties Londonderry, Tyrone and Fermanagh, which were densely settled by farmers in the seventeenth century. There is thus no simple form of repartition that will resolve the problem. It would be relatively easy to adjust the present border to exclude some areas of high Catholic density such as those parts of Derry that lie west of the River Foyle, South Armagh and certain other parts of counties Fermanagh and Tyrone adjoining the border. That was the approach pursued by the Boundary Commission and initially agreed to by the Irish representative in 1925.[10] Such a decision would presumably please nationalists living in those areas. But it would leave a very substantial Catholic minority within the remaining territory of Northern Ireland. It has been calculated, on 1971 figures, that a minimal repartition of this kind would have transferred some 100,000 Catholics and 30,000 Protestants to the Republic (see Figure 3(ii)). To transfer all the districts with a Catholic majority of more than 55 per cent and Fermanagh, in which there would probably be a voting majority of nationalists, would on 1981 figures have transferred some 250,000 Catholics and some 140,000 Protestants (see Figure 3(ii)). To transfer all districts with a majority of Catholics adjacent to the border – though it may be doubted whether there would be a voting majority of nationalists in them all, given the larger proportion of Catholics below voting age and the fact that not all Catholics might vote for a transfer – would involve a transfer of some 300,000 Catholics and some 175,000 Protestants.[11] That would leave just over 1 million people, of whom three-quarters would be Protestant, in the new Northern Ireland. The larger the transfer of territory from Northern Ireland to the Republic, the larger would be the number and proportion of Protestants who would be unwillingly transferred to the Republic.

This suggests that the only satisfactory means of creating a more homogeneous Northern Ireland would be to arrange a fairly substantial exchange of population in border areas. The results of the 1981 census indicate that in some areas this is already happening. There has been a large exodus of Protestants from those parts of Derry on the west bank of the Foyle to the 'safer' and largely Protestant Waterside area on the east bank. There has been a corresponding, though less dramatic, increase in the proportion of Catholics in some other border districts – for example, from 71 to 74 per cent in Newry and Mourne, from 57 to 61 per cent in Strabane and from 52 to 54 per cent in Fermanagh between 1971 and 1981 – which has not been paralleled throughout the Protestant 'heartland'. This is probably due to a combination of demographic factors and 'voluntary' population movement of Protestants from border areas and of Catholics from predominantly Protestant areas. It would be possible to seek to speed up this process by a programme of resettlement for the mainly rural population in border areas. That would be difficult enough, given the deep-rooted commitment that most farmers have to retaining their ancestral lands. But it would still leave untouched the large urban

Figure 3

Population distribution in 1981 and possible repartitions

These maps show (i) the Catholic population as a proportion of the total population in each of the twenty-six district council areas based on the 1981 census, and (ii) two possible repartition lines, a marginal adjustment based on 1971 census figures, involving the transfer of some 100,000 Catholics and 30,000 Protestants to the Republic, and a more substantial transfer of all district council areas in which there might be expected to be a voting majority of nationalists based on 1981 figures.

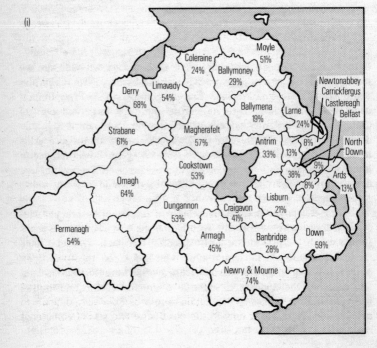

(ii)

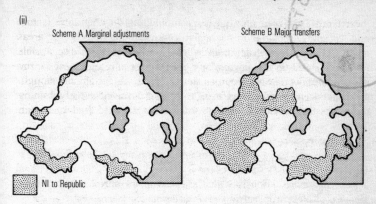

Scheme A Marginal adjustments   Scheme B Major transfers

NI to Republic

Note: These charts are based on allocations of those who refused to state their religion in the 1971 and 1981 censuses made by Dr Paul Compton of the Department of Geography, Queen's University, Belfast; the 1971 allocation was published in D. Watt (ed.), *The Constitution of Northern Ireland: Problems and Prospects* (London: Heinemann, 1981); the 1981 allocations have been supplied by Dr Compton from a more detailed analysis to be published in the near future.

Catholic population of Belfast and its surrounding towns. Since there are not enough urban Protestants in the towns of Tyrone, Fermanagh and South Armagh to balance these, a thoroughgoing exchange of population could not be achieved without transferring very large numbers of Catholics to towns and cities already in the Republic, and it is highly doubtful whether such a transfer would be either practicable or acceptable to the Republic. In any event no such transfers would be permissible in international law without the consent of those involved. Even with large financial inducements it is unlikely that consent would be forthcoming on any significant scale.

It is easy to see, in the light of this brief analysis of the practicalities of repartition, why neither the British nor the Irish Government has shown much interest in the idea. Marginal transfers, while desirable in themselves, would make no substantial impact on the underlying problem and might serve only to inflame passions within Northern Ireland and to whet the appetite of extreme nationalists. More substantial transfers and exchanges of population would be extremely difficult to achieve and might result only in the creation of two sets of embittered refugees.

Unilateral British Withdrawal

Faced with this seemingly endless list of straightforward and sensible solutions that will not work, many people in Britain and many foreign observers may come to the conclusion, if they have not already done so, that the only possible alternative to soldiering on indefinitely with an insoluble problem is a unilateral British withdrawal.[12] That is the only way, it is argued, to force the two communities in Northern Ireland to come to their senses and settle their differences. It is also the only way, some may add, to force the Protestant community to realize that it has long since lost the sympathy of the country to which it claims to be loyal and to negotiate seriously with the Government of the Republic as to the terms for eventual unification or federation.

These too are initially attractive arguments, even to those who are reluctant to concede victory to a terrorist campaign. But it is important, before accepting them, to give some thought to what is likely to happen if they are accepted.

The most likely response on the part of the Protestant community in Northern Ireland to a unilateral British withdrawal or to a declaration of intent to withdraw would be to mobilize itself in defence of its territory. That is what it did in 1912, in 1920 and in 1972, when the British Government suspended the Stormont Parliament. On each occasion tens of thousands of ordinary Protestants joined official or unofficial para-military bodies – the original Ulster Volunteer Force in 1912, the 'A', 'B' and 'C' Specials in the 1920s and the Ulster Defence Association in 1972. Both in the early 1920s and in the early 1970s substantial numbers of innocent Catholics were murdered. There is no reason at all to believe or hope, as the Provisional IRA and its supporters appear to, that it would be different in the 1980s.

What would happen next would depend largely on the response of the Catholic community in Northern Ireland and of the Government in the Republic. One possibility would be a huge increase in recruitment to the IRA and other similar bodies and a rapidly escalating civil war. Given the fact that there are already some 20,000 armed Protestants in the RUC, the RUC Reserve and the UDR (see above) and that the majority of the licensed rifles and shotguns in Northern Ireland are in the hands of Protestants, it is hard to see how the Catholics could win any serious confrontation. The more likely result would be the establishment of a provisional Protestant Government in Belfast and an untidy and bloody redrawing of the boundary between areas of Protestant and Catholic domination. There would also be likely to be an exodus of large numbers of Catholic refugees from Belfast to Dundalk and other border towns. The violence might spread to large British cities in which there are many Irish Catholics and Protestants, notably Liverpool and Glasgow.

Another possibility is that the Government of the Republic would send the Irish Army into Northern Ireland, with or without support from the United Nations (UN), in an attempt to restore order. Such a force could probably impose itself, given the superior fire power that it could command. But it would face a long and unrewarding guerrilla campaign and repeated demands for the granting of the right of self-determination to the northern Protestants. So too would a UN peacekeeping force of the kind that is often blithely advocated. Direct UN involvement in other comparable conflicts has not prevented bloodshed or political disintegration. The typical role of UN peacekeeping forces has been to police a political graveyard rather than to save divided communities from themselves.

Perhaps the most likely course of events would be the tacit acceptance by the Republic and by most northern Catholics of the right of the northern majority to establish a new, though smaller, state and a brief period of disturbance and forced reallocation of population in border areas. This would not, of course, solve the problem. It would merely recreate the conditions that were created in the 1920s and would set the scene for the continuation of conflict in the new Northern Ireland.

It is hardly surprising, in this light, that no British or Irish Government has accepted the case for unilateral withdrawal. The risks of doing so are simply too great and the prospects of achieving a peaceful and stable settlement, even at the cost of some disruption and bloodshed, too small for any responsible Government to contemplate them. It is also arguable that it would be a breach of international law for the British Government to abrogate its responsibilities in Northern Ireland by any form of unilateral withdrawal against the wishes of the majority of the population. There is no precedent other than in Nazi Germany and South Africa for the expulsion and arbitrary denationalization of large numbers of loyal, if aggravating, citizens. Nor could the forcible transfer of territory to another state against the wishes of the majority of its inhabitants be justified in contemporary international law.[13]

A Better Way Forward

It is not necessary, in the face of these depressing facts and arguments, to conclude that there is no alternative to soldiering on with direct rule and searching for some form of compromise between the two communities that would allow the re-establishment of some form of regional government in Belfast. The rejection of joint authority of the kind proposed by the New Ireland Forum (see above) does not mean that all talk of shared arrangements between Britain and the Republic or Northern Ireland and the Republic must be abandoned. Many of the drawbacks to the Forum model of joint authority can be avoided by adopting an approach to shared arrangements that cannot be portrayed either as a substantial step towards unification or as a denial of the aspiration for unification.

This was the strategy of the majority of the members of the Kilbrandon Committee, an unofficial all-party body set up in 1984 to give a considered British response to the Forum Report. The whole Committee accepted the need for some formal recognition by the Republic of the separate constitutional status of Northern Ireland as part of the United Kingdom as a precondition to unionist consent to any new arrangements. The majority of its members then favoured a form of joint authority, which they called 'co-operative devolution'. This would involve the appointment of a five-member ministerial executive made up of one British Minister, one Irish Minister and three representatives from Northern Ireland elected by proportional representation, two of whom would be expected to be unionist and one nationalist. This would enable the British and unionist members to prevail where they agreed but would remove the blocking power of unionists on measures agreed by the other three members. Legislative power on matters reserved for Northern Ireland might then be granted to an inter-parliamentary body with members from the Dáil and the House of Commons and perhaps also from a directly elected Northern Ireland Assembly, which might itself be granted direct control of certain local government functions.

These suggestions make more practical sense than the essentially colonial structures envisaged by the Forum Report. But the Kilbrandon majority itself foresaw the difficulty that if international responsibility for Northern Ireland were reserved for the British Government, it might insist on a general power of veto. It also seems highly unrealistic to expect unionists either to agree to participate in such a system, given their committed objection to power-sharing with Republicans even within Northern Ireland, or to accept its imposition without their participation.

The work of the Kilbrandon Committee none the less points the way towards a new framework for Northern Ireland that recognizes the rights of the nationalist minority and meets the need for functional co-operation with the Republic in ways that do not threaten the rights of the unionist majority. If the basic problem over the legitimacy of Northern Ireland can be resolved, a whole range of possible structures may be explored through which powers and functions can be shared between Britain and Ireland and between Northern Ireland and the Republic without necessarily granting to the Republic any unilateral authority over Northern Ireland. In such a framework no detailed blue-print is required. As within the larger framework of the European Community, the potential for strengthening common and reciprocal arrangements must be left to the states and peoples involved. The basic framework for an approach of this kind will be outlined in the next chapter. Some possible arrangements for recognizing the rights and interests of the two communities within Northern Ireland and for co-operation between Northern Ireland and the Republic and between the Republic and Britain will then be discussed in greater detail in the remaining chapters.

3
A New Framework: Reflecting the Realities

Most of the solutions that have been discussed in Chapter 2 are based on the assumption that one or other of the two communities in Northern Ireland can be enticed, persuaded or coerced into abandoning its historic identity and allegiance. The essential reason why these solutions cannot be expected to work is that both communities have shown themselves to be remarkably resilient in maintaining their separate identities and allegiances. Since, as will be explained, there is no reason to expect that the social and economic factors that explain this resilience can be changed in the foreseeable future, the only practicable alternative is to seek a framework for resolving the Northern Ireland problem that acknowledges the realities of the situation.

This was probably the true message of the New Ireland Forum, however much it may have been obscured by the emphasis in the Forum Report on its three preferred options. Following the publication of the Forum Report two of the leading participants, Garret Fitzgerald and John Hume, have repeatedly focused attention on the 'realities and requirements' listed in the Report and on the offer to discuss any other proposals that 'may contribute to political development' (para. 5.10). That serious discussions are still being pursued between the British and Irish Governments, despite the summary rejection of all three Forum options by the British Prime Minister and two successive Secretaries of State for Northern Ireland, Jim Prior and Douglas Hurd, is as good an indication as any of the fact that two of the three were no more than restatements of the aspiration for Irish unity and that the third, joint authority, was an initial negotiating position.

Realities and Requirements

The realities and requirements identified in the Forum Report are concerned primarily with the situation in Northern Ireland – the need to accept the separate identities, cultures and aspirations of the two communities and to recognize their legitimacy in any settlement (paras 5.1 and 5.2) (see Appendix). In the Forum Report these were naturally seen in an exclusively Irish context. But there are other realities and requirements that stem from geography and from the historical and present relationship between Britain and Ireland. Eight hundred years of governmental unity in one form or another have created ties that cannot be ignored. There has always been a significant interchange of population between the two islands. The Norman invasion in the twelfth century and the deliberate plantation of English and Scots settlers in Ireland during the seventeenth century created throughout Ireland a distinct Anglo-Irish community, which has been partially, but not wholly, integrated in the Republic and which has maintained a very distinct identity in Ulster. There is an equally large Irish population in Britain, resulting mainly from the very high level of emigration in the nineteenth and early twentieth centuries. This flow of population in both directions still continues, though at a lower level. It has created over the years a significant degree of common culture, not just in language and literature but also in sport, in the media, in education, in the structures of law and government and in ordinary consumer experience. Ireland is different from Britain. But it is not very different.

These realities have been reflected at a mundane level since the Republic became independent in 1921. There has always been freedom of movement and settlement between the two islands, limited only by the provisions of the Prevention of Terrorism Act. The two countries share a common system for the control of aliens and neither treats the other's citizens as such. Irish citizens have long been entitled to vote in British elections, and a similar right is to be granted to British citizens in Ireland. The British Isles – or 'these islands' as people in the Republic prefer to call them – are an integrated unit for postal charges and share a common system for professional and technical education in many spheres. All these and many other similar arrangements pre-date the links established through common membership of the European Community and might be considered anomalous in international law. But no one regards them as anything but a reasonable and pragmatic recognition of our common heritage.[1]

43

Contradictory Claims

This realism and flexibility has not until recently been extended to the Northern Ireland problem. Both states have instead made a practice of asserting contradictory and highly unrealistic claims. Since 1937 the Republic has asserted a formal, though not a practical, claim to exercise jurisdiction over Northern Ireland in Articles 2 and 3 of its Constitution. The controversial and ambiguous nature of these notorious articles can be savoured only by reading the full text:

Art. 2 *The national territory consists of the whole island of Ireland, its islands and territorial seas.*

Art. 3 *Pending the reintegration of the national territory, and without prejudice to the right of the Parliament and Government established by this Constitution to exercise jurisdiction over the whole of that territory, the laws enacted by that Parliament shall have the like area and extent of application as the laws of Saorstat Éireann (i.e. the twenty-six counties of the Republic) and the like extra-territorial effect.*

The adoption of these provisions had more to do with the internal politics of the Republic than anything else. Their precise legal effect is debatable. The claim to sovereignty over the entire island is dubious in international law, not least because the Republic has hardly been energetic in pursuing it. It has been argued by lawyers in the Republic that they amount to no more than a statement of the aspiration to unity.[2] But their intended purpose and actual effect have been very different. They are seen by northern unionists as a direct denial of the legitimacy of Northern Ireland. And in the aftermath of the Sunningdale agreement of December 1973 they were relied on for precisely that purpose in a test case, *Boland* v. *An Taoiseach*, organized by opponents of Sunningdale in the Republic. The judges in the Supreme Court held that the declaration made by the Government of the Republic accepting the current status of Northern Ireland (see below) was not unconstitutional, since it amounted at most to a *de facto* rather than a *de jure* recognition of Northern Ireland as part of the United Kingdom.[3] But two judges also indicated that if it had amounted to an agreement on fact or principle, it might have infringed Articles 2 and 3. This was quite enough to give powerful political ammunition to Ian Paisley and other opponents in Northern Ireland of the power-sharing Executive that owed its existence to the Sunningdale accord.

The British Government for its part began in the 1920s by abdicating all responsibility for what happened in Northern Ireland to the northern unionists. When it was forced to resume effective responsibility in 1969 it went to the other extreme by repeatedly asserting its absolute and exclusive jurisdiction over Northern Ireland and by refusing to acknowledge in any way that the nationalist minority had not been adequately consulted about the creation of Northern Ireland or that its identity and interests had not been properly protected in the arrangements for the government of the province. Both in its legislation and in its governmental practice Britain seemed always to recognize the rights – and the right of veto – only of the unionist majority. The terms of the notorious 'guarantee' to unionists first given under the Ireland Act 1949 (s. 1(2)) must also be savoured in full:

> It is hereby declared that Northern Ireland remains part of His Majesty's dominions and of the United Kingdom and it is affirmed that in no event will Northern Ireland or any part thereof cease to be part of His Majesty's dominions and of the United Kingdom without the consent of the Parliament of Northern Ireland.

Although this reassurance to the unionist majority was an understandable response to the decision by the Irish Government in 1948 to repudiate the vestiges of the link with Britain by leaving the Commonwealth and declaring a republic, it was viewed by the nationalist minority as a ratification of Unionist Party misrule and as yet more proof of its own irrelevance to British thinking. The amendment of this guarantee under the Northern Ireland Constitution Act 1973, following the suspension of the Stormont Parliament, to read 'without the consent of the majority of the people of Northern Ireland voting in a poll' (s. 1) merely served to confirm this view. Though the guarantee is as irrelevant both in strict law and for practical purposes as Articles 2 and 3 of the Irish Constitution, its apparent acceptance of a unionist veto on all constitutional change makes it as offensive to nationalists as those articles are to unionists.[4]

Over the years the two communities in Northern Ireland have reacted in an entirely predictable way to these conflicting approaches on the part of their sponsors in Britain and the Republic. Unionists have typically refused to have anything to do with the Republic until it withdraws its claim to jurisdiction over Northern Ireland and recognizes the legitimacy of their state. They fear, irrationally but understandably, that until full legitimacy is conceded, any all-Ireland arrangements and any concession to the minority will merely be the first of a series of steps towards unification. Nationalists have typically refused to participate fully in any system of government within Northern Ireland that does not explicitly recognize in some institutional way the legitimacy of their claim to be part of the Irish nation. They too may be excused for fearing that to do so would help to give stability to a state that has not yet granted them any real recognition. The failure by the Republic and by Britain to agree and commit themselves fully to a single view on the constitutional status of Northern Ireland and on the legitimate rights of the majority and minority communities there has thus been a major barrier to successive attempts to find a workable and generally acceptable system of government for it. It may even be claimed that the Sunningdale agreement in 1973 and the power-sharing Executive that it created in 1974 failed precisely because the internal arrangements within Northern Ireland were set up before the two states had worked through the full implications for their own relationships and commitments.

All of this was avoidable. There was an opportunity first in 1921, on the signature of the original treaty between Britain and Ireland, and more clearly in 1925, when the Boundary Commission collapsed and a further treaty was signed, for the two states to make realistic provisions for the protection of their respective minorities on either side of the accepted border.[5] But apart from the provision of constitutional prohibitions against discrimination, which were to prove wholly inadequate, the problem was ignored.[6] The Republic took refuge in the rhetoric of anti-partition. The British took refuge in the comfortable feeling that their provision in 1920 for a kind of federal home rule for Ireland, in which both Northern and Southern Ireland would share certain functions in a Council of Ireland, had been thwarted by intransigence on both sides. As a result they left the northern unionists to manage the nationalist minority in whatever way they pleased.

It cannot seriously be argued that either side was unaware of its obligations. Following the war of 1914–18 new boundaries had been drawn all over Europe, and many new national and linguistic minorities had been created. The protection of minorities within these new states was a central concern of the major powers at the time, including Britain, and elaborate guarantees were established through a series of treaties under the supervision of the League of Nations.[7] Little thought appears to have been given to making analogous arrangements in the treaties of 1921 and 1925.

The obligations of the two states have not diminished in any way over the intervening years. Both Britain and Ireland are active members of the United Nations, which has also turned its attention to the problem of protecting minorities. In the Capotorti Report, prepared for the United Nations Subcommission on the Prevention of Discrimination and the Protection of Minorities and finally published in 1979, the desirability of bilateral treaties between states most directly concerned was stressed:

> *History shows that the minority problem can poison international relations.*
> *However, with the new standards set by the United Nations in the*
> *framework of human rights, minority groups can now play a positive role in*
> *international relations. When their rights are guaranteed and fully respected*
> *minority groups can serve as a link between States. The Special Rapporteur*
> *strongly believes that bilateral agreements dealing with minority rights*
> *concluded between States where minorities live and the States from which*
> *such minorities originate (especially between neighbouring countries) would*
> *be extremely useful. It must be stressed, however, that co-operation with*
> *regard to the rights of members of minority groups shall be based on mutual*
> *respect for the principles of the sovereignty and territorial integrity of the*
> *States concerned and non-interference in their internal affairs. (Para. 618,*
> *recommendation 10(b))*

It might be thought that this passage was written with Northern Ireland particularly in mind. It was not. The problems posed by drawing boundaries in areas of mixed population are common throughout the world. In this respect at least the Northern Ireland problem is no more intractable than many others, and the appropriate response is well-recognized.

Similar, though less precisely defined, obligations are imposed on Britain and Ireland by virtue of their membership of the European Community, which, like the United Nations, was established principally as a means of breaking down historic enmities. Member states are bound to recognize their existing boundaries and are expected, with the assistance of their fellow members, to resolve any outstanding difficulties by sharing resources across national frontiers and by channelling the potentially dangerous forces of traditional nationalism into a broader communal framework. Are the problems between Britain and Ireland in Northern Ireland any less difficult than those that arise on the border between France and Germany? Can they not also be resolved more effectively and permanently by co-operation than by the assertion of nineteenth-century notions of the nation state or by attempting to redraw established boundaries?

A New Anglo-Irish Treaty

These arguments suggest that the first requirement for resolving the Northern Ireland problem is a decision by the British and Irish states to realign their relationship over a territory that was once in dispute between them so as to emphasize current realities rather than historic enmities.

The only effective method of doing this would be the signing of a new Anglo-Irish treaty setting out the essentials of the approach that both states now accept.

To begin with, such a treaty should record the basic facts about the partition of Ireland and the creation of Northern Ireland as they have been explained above. It should then commit both states to the same fundamental principles in dealing with the resulting problem: first, that the state to which Northern Ireland belongs must be determined by a free and fair exercise in self-determination by all the people of Northern Ireland; and, second, that the rights, aspirations and interests of both communities within it must be guaranteed and monitored by both states with whatever international assistance may appropriately be sought.

In one sense this would not be a new departure. In the Sunningdale communiqué of December 1973 both states recited their acceptance of the first of these basic principles in the following parallel declarations:

The Irish Government fully accepted and solemnly declared that there could be no change in the status of Northern Ireland until a majority of the people of Northern Ireland desired a change in that status.	The British Government solemnly declared that it was, and would remain, their policy to support the wishes of the majority of the people of Northern Ireland. The present status of Northern Ireland is that it is part of the United Kingdom. If in future, the majority of the people of Northern Ireland should indicate a wish to become part of a united Ireland the British Government would support that wish.

These commitments have been repeated at successive Anglo-Irish summits by Governments headed both by Garret Fitzgerald and by Charles Haughey. The British Government for its part has added a more general acceptance of the validity of both the unionist and the nationalist identity in Northern Ireland, notably in the White Paper *A Framework for Devolution*,[8] presented by Jim Prior in 1982 in preparation for the re-establishment of the Northern Ireland Assembly. A corresponding recognition of the validity of the unionist tradition was made in the New Ireland Forum Report. Despite some preliminary studies under the auspices of the so-called Anglo-Irish Intergovernmental Council, established at the summit of 1980, however, little has been done to give practical or legal effect to these declarations. Successive Governments in both countries have preferred to work informally on matters of practical day-to-day concern rather than to face the more difficult issues. Neither state has yet been prepared to enter into a binding international agreement or to pass internal legislation to establish beyond all doubt the legitimacy of Northern Ireland and to clarify the respective rights and obligations of the two communities.

The registration of a new Anglo-Irish treaty at the United Nations, as was envisaged for the Sunningdale agreement in 1973, would confirm its status as an agreement between two equal and sovereign states acting in concord with none of the undertones of inequality, duress and discord that characterized the initial Anglo-Irish treaties. Such a treaty might also provide for some form of international supervision of its performance, notably through its incorporation in the respective constitutional and legal systems of the two states. In so far as the Republic is concerned, this would involve the reformulation of Articles 2 and 3 of the Irish Constitution. In so far as Britain is concerned, it would involve the enactment of a new Northern Ireland Constitution Act. In each case it would clearly be desirable that the basic principles should be expressed in identical words, so that the risk of future arguments on interpretation would be minimized.

Agreement by both Britain and the Republic on the fundamental principles of their approach to Northern Ireland, as indicated in the draft heads of a treaty given on pages 50–51, would remove one of the major barriers to creating a new relationship between the two communities in Northern Ireland, in that each is currently reluctant to make any concession that might prejudice its position in any future negotiations. It would facilitate the adoption of a series of measures designed to permit nationalists in Northern Ireland to express their Irish identity in ways that do not conflict with the status of Northern Ireland as part of the United Kingdom. This in its turn might facilitate the acceptance by both sides of a form of local administration in which both communities could play a part without requiring the highly unrealistic degree of consensus on all matters built into the power-sharing model that was tried but failed in 1974.

Acceptance of the legitimacy of Northern Ireland on the part of the Republic and the acknowledgement by Britain of the existence of an Irish community within Northern Ireland would also facilitate the creation of new formal structures for co-operation between Northern Ireland and the Republic. This might include the exercise of joint authority on specified matters on either side of the border on a reciprocal basis, thus avoiding some of the objections to the proposals in the Forum Report and the Kilbrandon Report for the imposition of joint authority by Britain and Ireland on all aspects of the government of Northern Ireland. The exercise of any authority over Northern Ireland by the Republic on a unilateral basis is inherently objectionable to unionists, since it implies that the Republic has a right to intervene. The exercise of authority by

49

DRAFT HEADS OF A TREATY BETWEEN THE UNITED KINGDOM AND THE REPUBLIC OF IRELAND

The Governments of the United Kingdom and of the Republic of Ireland

recognizing their commitments and responsibilities under the Charter of the United Nations, within the European Communities and within the Council of Europe, in particular under the European Convention on Human Rights and Fundamental Freedoms,

recognizing the special relationships which exist between their peoples, and the steps already taken to express those relationships in the Anglo-Irish Intergovernmental Council and other institutions,

recognizing that Northern Ireland is a territory in which there are two communities with divided loyalties and in which special arrangements are required to ensure that those loyalties can be fully expressed,

recognizing that the conflict in Northern Ireland has caused and continues to cause untold suffering to both its communities and that it poses a grave threat to the prosperity and to the democratic institutions of both countries,

recognizing that there is no democratic manner of determining which state the territory of Northern Ireland shall belong to other than by a plebiscite of its people,

recognizing that the two communities are entitled to equal respect and to equal treatment before the law,

recognizing that the arrangements adopted in 1920 and thereafter failed to give adequate respect and equal treatment to one of those communities,

HAVE THEREFORE RESOLVED

(1) to take further measures to secure the common concerns of their peoples, and to ensure co-operation and harmony in future relations without prejudice to the independence or the sovereign rights of both states;

(2) that there shall be no change in the constitutional status of Northern Ireland as part of the United Kingdom until a majority of the people of Northern Ireland desire a change;

(3) that appropriate measures [as discussed in Chapter 6] shall be taken by both states to guarantee the rights and interests of both communities in Northern Ireland and that if at any time in the future a majority of the people in Northern Ireland should vote to join a united Ireland, corresponding measures shall be taken by both states to guarantee the rights and interests of both communities within a unitary Irish state;

(4) that appropriate measures [as discussed in Chapter 7] shall be taken to develop co-operation between Northern Ireland and the Republic on matters of social, economic and cultural policy;

(5) that appropriate measures [as discussed in Chapter 8] shall be taken by both states to deal more effectively with terrorism;

(6) that appropriate measures shall be taken to give effect to this agreement in the domestic laws and constitutions of both states.

joint agencies on either side of the border on a reciprocal basis, as discussed below, has no such implications and emphasizes the equal legitimacy of both Northern Ireland and the Republic. Acceptance of a new co-operative relationship between Britain and the Republic would likewise make it possible to develop new formal structures to reflect that relationship. The need to monitor progress in the implementation of the more detailed provisions of a new treaty and to supervise the exercise of joint authority on a reciprocal basis would provide an obvious and essential function for the parliamentary tier of the Anglo-Irish Intergovernmental Council that has often been proposed.

These various ideas will be developed in greater detail in the chapters that follow. But it must be stressed that action will have to be taken at each of these three different levels to reflect new relationships between the two communities in Northern Ireland, new relationships between Northern Ireland and the Republic and new relationships between Britain and the Republic. It is for this reason that talk of an 'internal settlement' within Northern Ireland without reference to a prior 'external settlement' between Britain and Ireland is so unhelpful. It does not follow that progress at each of these levels will be equally easy to achieve or that all the elements of a new settlement are likely to be agreed and implemented within the same timescale. But there can be no question of seeking an internal settlement within Northern Ireland until the relations between Britain and the Republic have been put on a sound basis. Nor can there be much progress with respect to relations between Northern Ireland and the Republic until appropriate and workable structures for government within Northern Ireland have been established.

4
Northern Ireland: Why it Failed

Northern Ireland was created by the essentially pragmatic British decision to partition Ireland in 1920. It comprises about one-fifth of the area and one-third of the population of Ireland. It is a divided society in which two separate communities are locked in political conflict. The majority community is composed of almost 1 million Protestants, or unionists, who wish to remain British. The minority community is composed of more than half a million Catholics, or nationalists, who aspire to a united Ireland.*

Almost everyone now recognizes these basic facts, with the possible exception of some ill-informed Irish Americans who still believe that Northern Ireland is occupied by British troops against the will of the bulk of the population. But there is still a tendency to think that the divisions in Northern Ireland are due wholly to partition and the 'fifty years of unionist misrule' that followed it. As so often in Ireland, it is not quite as simple as that. The roots of the communal division go back far beyond partition. And the division is maintained by powerful social and economic forces that are too readily ignored by those who seek simple political

* There are obvious difficulties in using any of these common labels. Calling the two communities Protestant and Catholic suggests, wrongly, that the conflict is primarily religious (though religious intolerance, prejudice and bigotry are widespread in both communities) and ignores the large numbers on either side who do not practise any religion. Calling them unionist and nationalist is equally misleading, in that it suggests that the fairly substantial number of Catholics who are content to remain British have thereby ceased to be part of the minority community. And giving any single label to either community gives a false impression of unity and common purpose. There are huge differences between hard-line unionists – usually called loyalists – and liberal unionists, and between hard-line nationalists – usually called republicans – and other Catholics. Even to talk in terms of majority and minority communities is unsatisfactory in that it suggests that the boundary of Northern Ireland is immutable. Some of these subtle differences are reflected in the choice of one or other label in the text.

explanations and solutions. Anyone who wants to understand the Northern Ireland problem and to make a real contribution to resolving it must begin by understanding the historical foundation of the communal division and the way in which it is maintained in the ordinary lives of Ulster people.

The Two Communities: Where They Came From

The peculiar persistence of the communal division in Northern Ireland stems from the fact that the 'plantation' of British settlers there was a much more thorough job than elsewhere in Ireland. The Norman invasion of Ireland in the twelfth century merely imposed a foreign nobility on what was already a largely feudal native Irish society. The intention of later plantations was to create more peaceful and stable conditions by excluding the native or 'mere' Irish from large tracts of land and replacing them by loyal British settlers. The first attempt was made in the midland counties of Laois (Queen's County) and Offaly (King's County) under Queen Mary Tudor. This was followed by a fairly thin settlement in counties Cork and Kerry under Queen Elizabeth.

In Ulster, which had held out longest against British rule, the process began with an unofficial settlement of Scottish Presbyterians in the thinly populated north-eastern counties of Antrim and Down at the start of the seventeenth century. The Ulster Scots gradually took possession of the whole of these counties with the exception of the mountainous areas of Moyle in the north and Mourne in the south. Then after the failure of the Catholic rebellion of 1598–1603 and the eventual flight of the rebel Ulster earls in 1607, James I decided to settle the remaining Ulster counties. The intention was to exclude the native Irish Catholics altogether. In practice the Protestant settlers from England and Scotland took only the best land, mainly in the river valleys, leaving the Catholic Irish in possession of the hill country and other less desirable tenancies elsewhere. There they remained, a continual threat to the settlers' homesteads, despite the reinforcement of the settlement after the victorious British campaigns by Cromwell in 1649 and 1650 and by William of Orange in 1689 and 1690, culminating in the famous Battle of the Boyne, which is still celebrated by Orangemen on the Twelfth of July each year.

These victories ensured the permanence of the Protestant ascendancy in Ulster. The settlers and the dispossessed Catholics none the less continued their skirmishes throughout the seventeenth and eighteenth centuries. Towards the end of the eighteenth century a number of secret

54

societies, notably the Orange Order, were formed on either side for mutual protection and revenge. When physical violence became less common, the struggle for land in rural areas continued at every land sale or inheritance. Farming land even now rarely passes from one community to the other. In the towns the balance between the two communities was only a little more flexible. Catholics were permitted to establish themselves in the cathedral cities of Derry, Armagh, Omagh, Newry and Downpatrick, where they still predominate, though the Protestants typically control the hinterland. The situation was reversed in a few predominantly Protestant towns, like Cookstown and Enniskillen, which were deliberately established in predominantly Catholic areas. In Belfast the proportion of Catholics grew rapidly in the early nineteenth century as the factory system developed and reached a peak of 34 per cent in 1861.

These patterns may be traced fairly accurately from the midnineteenth century when regular censuses began to be taken. Since then the proportions of the two communities have remained remarkably stable. In the counties of Antrim and Down Protestants have long outnumbered Catholics by four or five to one. In Belfast the proportion has stabilized at about two to one. In the counties of Londonderry and Armagh there has been a continuing small majority of Protestants and in Tyrone and Fermanagh a small majority of Catholics.

The position in the rest of Ireland was always very different. In the remaining Ulster counties of Donegal, Monaghan and Cavan the 1901 census recorded only one Protestant for every three or four Catholics. In Dublin and the relatively well-settled counties of Wicklow, Wexford and Carlow there was only one Protestant for every four or five Catholics, and elsewhere there were more than ten Catholics for every one Protestant. Since partition in 1920 the proportion of Protestants in the Republic has declined still further. To begin with there was a mass exodus of Protestants. Between 1911 and 1926 their numbers declined by more than one-third. Thereafter the decline continued at a slower but fairly constant rate of about 10 per cent each decade until the 1970s, when it halted.

How They Maintain Themselves

How and why have the two communities in Northern Ireland, in contrast to the Republic, maintained themselves with so little change over the years? The basic answer is that both communities have kept themselves

55

to themselves, and that each is large enough and sufficiently concentrated to sustain its natural growth. The greater natural growth in the Catholic community has then been offset by a higher level of emigration, which in turn may be linked with established patterns of employment and unemployment.

The process of segregation begins with education. There are two entirely distinct school systems in Northern Ireland, a state system and an independent Catholic system. Although the state schools are officially and legally non-sectarian, they are in practice Protestant, partly because virtually no Catholics go to most of them and partly because their management committees are composed largely of representatives of the Protestant Churches, whose independent schools were in effect taken over by the state system. The Catholic schools, which now receive virtually the same level of state funding as state schools, are expressly committed to educating their pupils in the Catholic faith and ethos and therefore have virtually no Protestant pupils. The teachers in the two sets of schools are, of course, recruited almost exclusively from one or other community, and there are two separate systems of teacher training. In a few of the better-known grammar schools there is some mixing of the two communities, though for the most part this is limited to a minority of relatively well-off Catholics who send their children to state or independent schools that are essentially Protestant. There is only one truly integrated secondary school, Lagan College, and that was founded only in 1982. Higher education, both in the universities and in technical and other professional colleges, on the other hand, is totally integrated. But by the time they reach higher education most children have already absorbed one or other of the two communal views of the history and legitimacy of Northern Ireland and of British involvement in Ireland as a whole, both through formal teaching and through their families and friends.

The separation of the two communities extends to many other aspects of daily life.[1] Most marriages, of course, are between members of the same community. Considerable family and social pressures are brought to bear against those who dare to embark on a 'mixed marriage'. Most leisure activities, particularly in rural areas, are arranged by the Churches and their associated organizations. There are even two distinct sporting systems. Catholics are encouraged to play Gaelic football and hurley. Protestants are encouraged to play standard British games, like football, rugby and cricket. Trades and professions are similarly divided. Most Catholics attend Catholic doctors and dentists, consult Catholic solicitors and accountants and employ Catholic tradesmen. Most Protestants attend Protestant doctors and dentists, consult Protestant solicitors and accountants and employ Protestant tradesmen. In smaller towns and in the suburbs of bigger towns many small shops are identified as providing principally for one or other community, even where there is little physical segregation. All this is designed to support as full a range of jobs and services as possible within each community. It has the effect of minimizing contacts between them. It is perfectly possible, and quite normal, to live a full and varied life in Northern Ireland without having any real contact with people from the other community.

The separation cannot be complete. In larger factories and shops and in public employment there is a good deal of mixing. But even in these sectors there are well-established patterns.[2] Until recently recruitment in engineering, one of the staple industries of Belfast, was almost exclusively Protestant. Banking and insurance were also largely Protestant. Employment in the construction industry and in hotels and catering and the drink trade, on the other hand, has long been predominantly Catholic. In the public sector, as will be seen, there was (and in some areas still is) a sufficient difference in the proportion of Protestants and Catholics to warrant allegations of deliberate or tacit discrimination. These patterns are also reflected within the trade union movement, despite its claim to be above the sectarian divisions. In some cases, like teaching, there are two entirely separate unions. In others the predominantly Protestant or Catholic membership is reflected by affiliation with British or with Irish parent unions respectively.

These examples – and many more could have been given – show the extent to which Northern Ireland really is a divided society. This is not just a question of social segregation and economic differentiation. The two communities have entirely different views of the world in which they live. The nationalist community sees Ireland as a natural geographical and political unit that has a right to be independently governed. The unionist community sees nothing wrong with the partition of Ireland and the continuing link with Britain. The nationalist community thinks of itself as part of the Irish nation, which is regarded as Catholic, Gaelic and essentially non-British. The unionist community feels itself to be excluded from that kind of Irish nation and clings all the harder to its British, or non-Irish, identity. There are equally different perceptions of what might be thought to be factual matters. Unionists typically deny that there is any real differentiation or discrimination in employment patterns and regard statistics that indicate otherwise as suspect or biased. Many nationalists contest the accuracy of the latest census figures on the relative strength of the two communities. Both communities have entirely different perceptions of the causes of the recent 'troubles' and of what has actually happened in a long series of disputed incidents and security operations.

This does not mean that Ulster people spend their time arguing, abusing each other or fighting. On the contrary, they are naturally polite. But they are also naturally reserved and wary on first acquaintance. That is because it is important for them to establish on which side someone else stands. When two Ulster people whose communal identity is not self-evident meet, each immediately sets about discovering – without, of course, asking – whether the other is Protestant or Catholic. Since the difference between members of the two communities is not instantly apparent, as it would be in societies divided by race, colour or language, they use a series of more or less accurate cues: surnames (some disclose likely communal identity, some do not); Christian names (Catholics tend to use Irish-sounding names, while Protestants do not); schooling (perhaps the best guide if it can be got at); the 'h' test (Catholics tend to say 'haitch', while Protestants tend to say 'aitch'); or just the attitudes that may be disclosed on a whole range of sensitive issues. The point of this elaborate process is to enable both parties to avoid saying or revealing something that may prove embarrassing or offensive or may lead to disagreement on some fundamental issue. The desire to avoid having to embark on an argument that both sides know cannot be resolved is as good an indication as any of the stubbornness with which each clings to its basic political beliefs.

The Stormont Regime –
Fifty Years of Sectarian Politics

The communal division in Ulster did not begin with partition. Sectarian strife was endemic in rural areas throughout the eighteenth century. Belfast was notorious for its sectarian employment practices and for its sectarian riots throughout the nineteenth century. The political interests and commitments of the two communities were similarly opposed to each other long before partition was thought of. With the exception of a brief period at the end of the eighteenth century when dissenters and Catholics joined forces as United Irishmen against the British establishment, the Ulster Protestants, like the rest of the Anglo-Irish, could be relied on by the British authorities to assist in the suppression of Catholic unrest or rebellion. The opponents of Gladstone's original Home Rule Bill played the 'Orange Card' with devastating effect in 1886. The political differences between the two communities became much more important after the creation of Northern Ireland in 1920. Though the northern unionists had not originally wanted a separate state of their own, they accepted the 1920 settlement and soon grew to like the power that it gave them. From then on the sectarian divisions were not just a peripheral problem in a wider political context. They became the life blood of politics in a state that one side wished to maintain and the other to dismantle.

The first task of the Unionist Party Government inaugurated in Belfast in 1921 was to establish its authority throughout the six counties in the face of a continuing guerrilla campaign by the IRA and other irregulars. It was given a more or less free hand by the British Government to raise its own local forces to replace the British Army as it withdrew.[3] Three separate forces – the 'A', 'B' and 'C' Specials – were created to supplement the newly formed Royal Ulster Constabulary, which took over from the all-Ireland Royal Irish Constabulary. Legal authority for the arrest and internment of suspects was provided first under the Restoration of Order in Ireland Act 1920, which continued the wide powers conferred on the British forces under the wartime Defence of the Realm Regulations, and then under the Civil Authorities (Special Powers) Act (NI) 1922. In the period from 1921 to 1924 some 2,000 suspects were interned without trial. Between June 1920 and June 1922 over 400 people were killed,[4] either by the security forces or by irregular paramilitaries on either side. But armed resistance to the new state soon subsided, not least because the attention of the IRA was diverted to the much more intense civil war that broke out in the Republic in 1923. The Special Powers Act – to give it its popular name – was none the less kept in force and was used from time to time to intern republican activists, notably during the renewed IRA campaigns in 1938 and from 1956 to 1962.

The new regime faced a similar challenge on the political front. Most nationalists refused to have anything to do with the institutions of the new state. This caused particular problems in local government districts in which nationalists had a voting majority. To begin with the Unionist Government had to make temporary arrangements for the administration of a few such districts in which nationalist councillors voted to secede and refused to carry out their normal duties. In the longer term it sought to resolve this problem by redrawing local government boundaries in sensitive areas so as to produce unionist majorities in areas which nationalists might otherwise have controlled. The most blatant examples of this kind of gerrymandering were in Derry City and County Fermanagh.[5] In most local government areas, however, there were sufficient Unionist Party voters, given the relatively restricted local government franchise at that time and the fact that a higher proportion of the Catholic population has always been below voting age, to make any form of gerrymandering unnecessary. In elections for the Stormont Parliament the Unionist Party was content to rely on its natural voting strength, which regularly produced about forty MPs out of a total of just over fifty, and to permit the nationalists to hold the remaining seats. The decision by the Unionist Government in 1929 to repeal the proportional representation system of voting, which had been guaranteed under the 1920 settlement for a minimum period of three years,[6] was designed to limit possible fragmentation of the Unionist Party vote and the development of any form of alternative opposition, notably the Labour Unionists, rather than to reduce the number of nationalist MPs.

The most serious and continuing political concern of the unionists was the fear that the nationalist population would grow faster than their own. Given the higher Catholic birth rate and the explicit reliance on this prospect by some nationalists, the concern was a real one. The underlying unionist strategy was to ensure as far as was possible that job opportunities were reserved for Protestants and that the higher Catholic birth rate would be offset by emigration. In the private sector no governmental action was needed, since most Protestant employers – and most employers were Protestant – could be relied on to favour members of their own community. But the Government was able to ensure that new state-assisted industry was located in unionist areas. In the public sector the situation was essentially the same. Any form of legislative discrimination would have been clearly unlawful under the Government of Ireland Act 1920. But the Unionist Party was in a position, at both central and local government levels, to ensure that Protestants were appointed to most jobs and that Catholics were excluded from key positions. The reluctance of many Catholics to apply for, or to accept, official employment in a state that they preferred not to recognize was an additional advantage from this point of view, which the Government did nothing to counteract. It has been estimated that in 1971, after fifty years of Unionist Party rule, the unemployment rate among Catholics was more than double that among Protestants.[7]

In other matters the Unionist Government adopted an essentially conservative approach in avoiding state interference on matters of social and economic policy. But they accepted that in some matters, notably social security and welfare benefits, it was desirable to keep in step with British legislation. They were encouraged in this 'step-by-step' approach by an agreement with the British Government that any extra costs would be funded by a British subsidy. Both the law and administrative practice on most issues in which there was no direct communal interest on either side were thus kept broadly in line with the rest of Britain. On matters of this kind Northern Ireland was administered with reasonable efficacy. But nothing was done to heal the communal divisions or to encourage members of the minority community to become involved in the processes of government. The only serious attempt at removing one of the causes of the communal division, a scheme for integrated education which was proposed in the 1920s, was dropped in the face of combined opposition from both Protestant and Catholic Churches. On the contrary, the Government from time to time adopted measures that, though relatively unimportant in themselves, were clearly designed to emphasize that the assertion of any form of Irish identity on the part of the minority was illegitimate. The best examples were the prohibition of the naming of streets in Irish in 1949 and the Flags and Emblems (Display) Act 1954, which was intended to prevent the display of the Irish tricolour, though it did not formally prohibit it. In addition the Unionist Party worked hand in glove with successive controllers of the BBC in Belfast to ensure that the Irish identity of a large section of the community was ignored and a false sense of provincial harmony conveyed to the rest of the United Kingdom.[8]

The effects of this negative and sectarian approach to government on the part of the Unionist Party were entirely predictable. The bulk of the Catholic community felt itself to be excluded totally from any prospect of sharing in the government of the province and to be discriminated against both in employment opportunities and in the expression of its aspirations to Irish unity. Most Catholics consequently continued to regard Northern Ireland as an illegitimate state. Their elected representatives either indulged in the politics of abstention or else continued to challenge the very existence of the state. This in its turn permitted the Unionist Party to portray all or most Catholics as inherently disloyal and thus to justify their exclusion from the processes of government and from certain types of employment. Successive election campaigns were turned into renewed trials of strength on the constitutional issue. The communal division that the unionists had inherited from the past was thus made worse rather than better, and the prospects for creating a stable, peaceful and lasting state in Northern Ireland were injured rather than improved.

The Republic – Independence Before Unity

The contribution made by the Republic to the failure of Northern Ireland is equally significant. The primary impulse of Irish nationalism has always been separation from Britain rather than unity of the island.[9] The Proclamation of the Irish Republic at the GPO in 1916 and its Declaration in 1919 following the landslide electoral victory for Sinn Féin in 1918 was the result of centuries of frustration with unequal treatment under British rule and of a conviction that only complete separation achieved by force of arms could ensure justice for the Irish nation. Independence therefore was primary even if its price was partition. The Government of Ireland Act of 1920, which was designed to give limited self-government to Ireland while maintaining overall British sovereignty, was rejected by Sinn Féin because it compromised the independence of the Republic declared in 1919. Yet the Act would have created not only two home rule Parliaments for Northern Ireland and Southern Ireland but also a Council of Ireland that was intended to be a vehicle for eventual political unity. When that rejection and the subsequent military struggle led to a new offer from Britain, in the Anglo-Irish Treaty of 1921, of dominion status similar to that of Canada the debates in the Dáil over its acceptance focused almost exclusively on the remaining symbols of British rule, including the oath of allegiance and the Crown as Head of State, and the resulting limitation of complete independence. Partition and the right of Northern Ireland to vote itself out of the Free State were hardly mentioned. The bitter civil war that was fought over the 1921 Treaty led to a victory for the pro-treaty party (later Fine Gael), which in effect ratified partition in the Treaty of 1925. Those who lost the civil war split into a majority, led by de Valera, who were determined to fight by political means to undo the settlement of 1921 through the new party Fianna Fáil, and a minority who were committed to re-establishing the Republic by force of arms. It is to this rump of the independence forces of the 1920s that the Provisional IRA claims today to be the successor. When Fianna Fáil took power in 1932 it adopted a series of measures to move the state towards complete independence. This was finally achieved in 1948, when Ireland left the Commonwealth and declared itself a wholly independent republic. The point is not to criticize these efforts to assert identity and statehood, which blazed a path to be followed by many other former colonies after the Second World War. It is that they were pursued with little or no regard for their impact on the other national goal of uniting the people of North and South. Unity as a primary goal might well have dictated a wholly different approach to relationships between Britain and Ireland.

The internal policies adopted by successive Governments in the Republic are open to even more serious criticism. The Forum Report asserts that 'the constitutional, electoral and parliamentary arrangements in the South [in the 1920s] specifically sought to cater for the minority status of Southern Unionists and did so with considerable success' (para. 3.2). That is fair comment on the initial Constitution of the Irish Free State. It is not an accurate description of the policies and practices that were actually pursued in the Republic in respect of its Protestant minority. The credibility of the Forum Report would have been greatly increased by an honest acknowledgement that, allowing for the different size and circumstances of the minorities in both parts of Ireland after 1920, the record of intolerance and disregard for other than the majority interest was broadly similar both north and south of the border.

On social and religious issues the policies pursued since the 1920s progressively converted what might have been a pluralist state into a confessional state. Censorship of all literature that was offensive to the Catholic Church was imposed. The possibility of obtaining a divorce was eliminated. An explicitly Catholic Constitution was adopted in 1937. And many other laws and practices were adopted to give effect to the views of the Catholic majority regardless of those of the Protestant minority. In the cultural and educational sphere an exclusively Catholic and Gaelic, and often an anti-British, ethos was promoted. The numbers in the minority Protestant community declined very rapidly, both through emigration and through the rigid application of the Catholic Church's rules respecting the religion of children of mixed marriages. The 343,000 Protestants in the twenty-six counties of the Republic in 1901 had by 1961 declined to a mere 144,000.[10]

It is sometimes argued that these developments were an inevitable consequence of partition, which had created an overwhelming Roman Catholic majority in the South. But that is altogether too charitable a verdict on a state that ignored or overrode the values of the Protestant minority both within the twenty-six counties and within the thirty-two counties over which the Republic aspired to rule. While it was natural for a newly formed state to assert its independence from Britain and essential for it to create a distinctive cultural identity, the manner in which these aims were pursued reinforced the prejudices of the northern unionists and made their policies more difficult to criticize from within Northern Ireland and from without. When to the indisputable evidence that 'home rule' had in fact become 'Rome rule' is added the ambition expressed in Articles 2 and 3 of the Irish Constitution to incorporate Northern Ireland into the Republic, the substance of the criticism that the Republic carries its own responsibility both for the hostile nature of North–South relations and for the state of majority–minority relations within Northern Ireland is amply demonstrated.

The Decline and Fall of Stormont

The challenge that precipitated the decline and fall of the Stormont regime came from a somewhat unexpected quarter – not from the traditional nationalists against whom the unionists had prepared their defences but from the initially non-sectarian civil rights movement. During the 1960s things were getting better in Northern Ireland, as in the rest of Britain. The IRA campaign between 1956 and 1962 had not gained any widespread support among nationalists and had been easily contained. A new generation of relatively prosperous Catholics, who had benefited from the Northern Ireland version of Rab Butler's Education Act of 1944, was emerging from the schools and universities. Like many of their Protestant contemporaries, they rejected the barren sectarian politics of the Unionist and Nationalist parties alike. Their basic demand, like that of others in Europe who were influenced by the civil rights campaign by blacks in America, was for equal political and economic treatment for both communities within the established constitutional framework. In the Northern Ireland context attention was focused on inequalities in the local government franchise stemming from the failure of the Unionist Government to adopt post-war British reforms, the continuing existence of the Special Powers Act and the need for better provision and fairer allocation of jobs and housing.

The Unionist Government found it difficult to respond to demands of this kind in other than sectarian terms, despite the moves towards better relations with the Republic in the mid-1960s. The traditionalists in the party scented a republican plot and reacted accordingly. Marches and demonstrations by the Civil Rights Association were met by countermarches and demonstrations by extreme loyalists, led by the young Ian Paisley. The Government and the police fell back on a policy of attempting to ban civil rights marches. The rest of the story is familiar: escalating violence on the streets between civil rights campaigners and the police; the increasing involvement of loyalist mobs; the eruption of serious sectarian confrontations in the summer of 1969; the introduction of British troops in Derry and Belfast in an attempt to provide a more acceptable peacekeeping force; and the gradual re-emergence of the IRA in the role of defender of the Catholic community from attacks by loyalists and from repression by the security forces.

These events forced the British Government to abandon the policy, established in the 1920s, of avoiding any further involvement in the Irish question. To begin with it sought to limit its commitment to keeping the peace between the two communities and to putting pressure on the Unionist Government to carry through the reform programme set out in the Downing Street Declaration of August 1969. But it was gradually sucked into more detailed involvement both in political developments and in security. The resistance by the right wing of the Unionist Party to most of the reform programme meant that political pressure from London had to be maintained on a more or less continuous basis. And the increasing level of terrorist activity in addition to rioting on the streets made the integration of police and army operations of increasing importance.

This became particularly obvious when internment without trial was reintroduced in August 1971 at the insistence of the Unionist Government. The British Army was used in this operation to assist in the arrest and interrogation of large numbers of republican suspects chosen by the RUC Special Branch from out-of-date and inaccurate files that made little distinction between political and terrorist activists. The result was to unite the whole Catholic community in opposition to the Stormont regime and to increase both the flow of recruits to the IRA and the level of terrorist activity. In both the political and the security sphere the British Government was thus assuming greater responsibility without the formal power to impose its policies. The international outcry following the shooting dead of thirteen Catholic demonstrators in Derry on 30 January 1972 – 'Bloody Sunday' – finally led to a decision to impose direct control from London over all aspects of security and the administration of justice. When that was rejected by the Unionist Government, the Stormont regime was suspended in March 1972.

It is ironic that the fall of Stormont was brought about by the adoption by the British Government of the Unionist Government's policies of internment and a 'tough' approach to republican demonstrations. The more important question is whether the fall was inevitable or merely the result of a sectarian and ill-judged response to the demands of the civil rights movement. The experience of the British Government in attempting to deal with similar demands during more than twelve years of even-handed direct rule suggests that the incompetence and bias of the Unionist Party were not the only problem, but that a more fundamental reassessment of the nature of Northern Ireland is required.

5
Direct Rule: Why it has not Helped

The principal purpose of imposing direct rule from London was to replace the divisive Stormont regime by a patently fair and efficient system of government, both for security and for the distribution of governmental resources for housing, job creation and other such matters. In the short term it was hoped that this would reduce communal support for the IRA and other paramilitaries and increase the prospects of a ceasefire. In the longer term it was hoped that it would enable a new and more generally acceptable structure for devolved government to be established. After more than twelve years of direct rule neither of these objectives has been achieved. Why?

The answer given by the Forum Report is that the British Government has never got further than crisis management. That is unfair. Certain clearly defined policies have been consistently pursued: on the security front the policies of criminalization (treating terrorists as if they were ordinary criminals) and Ulsterization (handing over as much responsibility for security as possible to the locally recruited RUC and UDR); on the political front a policy of attempting to persuade local party leaders to agree on some form of internal 'power-sharing'; and on the socio-economic front measures to eliminate all forms of discrimination. The real problem is that none of these policies has worked because none of them has fully recognized the extent of the communal division in Northern Ireland and the need to accept the legitimacy of both traditions.

One Security Problem After Another

With hindsight it can be said that the main cause of the continuing violence in Northern Ireland has been the failure of the British Government to get to grips with the essentials of the political problem. But the security policies that it has pursued have undoubtedly made matters worse. The major failing in this sphere has been the apparent inability of the authorities to recognize and eliminate abuses in the operation of emergency powers. Since these abuses have been experienced mainly by the Catholic community, the result has been to increase the general lack of confidence in the administration of justice felt by many Catholics and to exacerbate their latent antagonism to any form of British rule. Though some of the more serious abuses have eventually been controlled, action has typically been taken after the damage has been done.[1]

One of the initial commitments of the British Government was the review of the Special Powers Act and the system of internment. A committee chaired by Lord Diplock was therefore appointed to recommend alternative means of dealing with terrorists. Diplock concluded[2] that there was no immediate practicable alternative to maintaining a system of 'detention' without trial, but that as many suspects as possible should be dealt with in special 'Diplock' courts, in which the risk of partisan verdicts would be avoided by the removal of the jury and in which the rules of evidence would be relaxed to allow convictions on the basis of confessions obtained during prolonged interrogation. This package was duly enacted in the Northern Ireland (Emergency Provisions) Act 1973. It did not prove any more effective or acceptable than the Special Powers Act. The new system of internment was used primarily in Catholic areas where the army was deployed, while the Diplock system was used primarily in Protestant areas where the RUC could operate more freely, although some loyalist paramilitaries were also interned. The army, in pursuit of military security tactics developed in Malaya, Kenya and other places, stretched its power to arrest and detain suspects to the limit in a system of mass screening in Catholic areas.[3] Thousands of ordinary people in republican areas were regularly arrested and questioned, and early morning 'head counts' were made on a street-by-street basis in order to build up a comprehensive intelligence record. This antagonized even those Catholics who opposed the IRA and made it possible for the IRA to sustain its recruitment and to maintain its operations despite the arrest and internment of hundreds of its members.

The second major review of emergency laws in Northern Ireland, chaired by Lord Gardiner, eventually recommended that internment could not be maintained as a long-term policy and that all terrorist suspects should be dealt with through the Diplock courts; Gardiner also recommended that the 'special category' status granted both to internees and to those convicted in Diplock courts should be phased out and that all convicted terrorists should be treated as ordinary criminals.[4] This policy of criminalization was implemented gradually. The last internee was released before Christmas in 1975. The privileges of special category status were denied to those convicted of offences committed after March 1976.

A new set of problems soon emerged. To begin with, the abandonment of internment led to increasing reliance on obtaining confessions from suspects during prolonged and intensive interrogation at two newly built interrogation centres at Castlereagh in Belfast and Gough Barracks in Armagh. Numerous complaints about ill-treatment and beatings during interrogation were initially ignored as mere propaganda. It was not until Amnesty International published a highly critical report in 1978 that the Government responded by appointing the Bennett Inquiry into interrogation procedures.[5] This led to the imposition of strict internal controls on interrogation practice, and complaints of this kind of ill-treatment declined dramatically.[6]

By 1978 another aspect of the criminalization policy began to create serious problems. Most IRA members convicted in Diplock courts after 1976 refused either to wear ordinary prison clothes or to work as directed. When they were denied their own clothes they refused to wear prison uniform and 'went on the blanket'. And when the authorities attempted to put pressure on them by refusing exercise and other facilities to the protesters, the prisoners retaliated by resorting to the so-called 'dirty protest' – smearing their cells with excrement. Finally in 1980 and 1981 there was a series of hunger strikes, the traditional and ultimate weapon of Irish protest. The apparent refusal of the Government to make any concessions, despite repeated pleas by successive Governments in the Republic, Church leaders and other intermediaries, again united a large section of the Catholic community in support of what seemed to them to be legitimate demands by those involved in political violence, even if they did not support the IRA. The extent of this support was clearly demonstrated by the election to Westminster of one of the hunger strikers, Bobby Sands, in the by-election in Fermanagh and South Tyrone in April 1981 and the election to the Dáil of two others, Kieran Doherty and Paddy Agnew, in the Republic in June 1981. The first two of these and eight others died in prison later that year, as did fifty others, both members of the security forces and civilians, caught up in the widespread rioting and violence sparked off by the hunger strikes. The Government was able to claim a victory of principle both over the dirty protest, in that the European Commission on Human Rights rejected the case taken by the protesters, and over the hunger strike, which was eventually abandoned. But the European Commission was highly critical of the 'inflexible approach' of the authorities, and many of the demands of the protesters, notably the right to wear their own clothes and a measure of segregation, were eventually conceded. There can be little doubt that a willingness on the part of the British Government to accommodate, if not formally to recognize, the determination of IRA members not to regard themselves as ordinary criminals would have spared Northern Ireland from one of the most bitter and polarizing crises of the present troubles and avoided a major boost for the morale and communal support of the Provisional IRA and its political counterpart, Provisional Sinn Féin.

The latest episode in the continuing saga of abuses in Diplock trials has been the systematic use of informers, or 'supergrasses', as they are popularly called. It seems likely that the difficulty experienced by the police in obtaining confessions following the introduction of the Bennett controls on interrogation caused them to seek informers not only to provide information, as all detectives do, but also to give evidence. Since known or suspected informers in Northern Ireland run a serious risk of being shot, those who agreed to co-operate had to be offered a safe and comfortable life after the trial and legal or practical immunity in respect of their own crimes. In 1982 and 1983 more than twenty informers were recruited in this way, and some hundreds of suspects were arrested and held for several years often on the sole evidence of the informer. When the first cases came to court almost all the defendants were convicted, usually without any corroboration of the informer's evidence. But as public disquiet has mounted the judges have taken a stronger line, and the evidence of a number of supergrasses has recently been rejected. As with internment and with interrogation, a legitimate weapon against terrorism – the use of informers' evidence when properly corroborated – has been discredited and devalued by its uncritical use and by a total failure on the part of the prosecuting authorities and the courts alike to insist on established safeguards.

Throughout the period of direct rule there has also been sporadic concern about the use of lethal force by members of the security forces. Figures produced for the New Ireland Forum indicated that of a total of 2,304 killings in Northern Ireland up to 1983, the security forces were responsible for at least 264.[7] Many such deaths have occurred in disputed circumstances. At times it has seemed as if special undercover units of the army or the police have been pursuing a policy of shooting suspected terrorists dead in order to avoid the difficulties of securing sufficient evidence to justify a court conviction. In 1978 ten suspects, of whom three turned out to be completely innocent, were shot dead by the army. In 1983 and 1984 seventeen persons were shot dead by the security forces, mostly in circumstances in which an arrest could probably have been safely effected. There have also been fifteen deaths from the use of supposedly non-lethal rubber and plastic bullets, and a number of other fatal incidents involving joy-riding and other street altercations. The response of the authorities to complaints about individual incidents is always to say that soldiers and policemen are subject to the ordinary law, that every case is carefully investigated and that a decision on whether to institute criminal proceedings is made by the independent Director of Public Prosecutions. In reality the Director is formally subject to the Attorney-General, who admitted in 1978 that such cases were discussed with him. Although some prosecutions have been initiated, almost all have resulted in acquittals. In addition the law on coroners' inquests in Northern Ireland is interpreted in such a way that in cases where there is no prosecution no public scrutiny of the evidence is made until several years after the event. Members of the minority community and many independent observers simply do not believe that the same rules are applied in cases involving the security forces as in other cases.

All of these practices, with the exception of the supergrass system, have been directed primarily against members of the Catholic community and have reinforced their instinctive lack of confidence in British security policies and in the British judicial system. The policy of Ulsterization has affected the situation in a rather different way. Since 1976 there has been a progressive shift from reliance on the army as the front-line force both against terrorists and in dealing with riots and civil disorder to reliance on the RUC and the UDR. In 1973, at the height of the 'troubles', there were some 16,500 (for a brief period up to 23,000) British troops in Northern Ireland, compared with some 14,500 local forces – 4,500 in the RUC, 2,500 in the RUC Reserve and 7,500 in the UDR. By 1984 there were some 20,000 local forces – 8,000 in the RUC, 4,500 in the RUC Reserve and 7,500 in the UDR – compared with at most 9,000 British troops. The winding down of the military security system in itself is clearly desirable. The difficulty is that all but some hundreds in the RUC and UDR are Protestants, partly because the IRA has made a point of murdering Catholics in the security forces and partly because most Catholics would not wish to join them in any case. The result is that one community has been given the task of policing the other and that the antagonism against many aspects of security policy felt by most Catholics has again become a communal and sectarian issue, as it was under the Stormont regime. Much of the hatred and distrust among Catholics is directed against the UDR, some of whose members have been found guilty of serious sectarian crimes. The anger in the Protestant community over the merciless IRA policy of killing UDR members, both on and off duty, has in turn increased the ill-feeling between the two communities.

These problems – the failure by the authorities to establish proper safeguards against the abuse of emergency powers and to ensure that disputed incidents are promptly investigated and properly dealt with and the unintended consequences of Ulsterization – have made even more difficult the task that lies ahead of building a police force and a judicial system in which reasonable members of both communities can place their trust. This in turn has exacerbated the problem of creating political institutions in which representatives of both communities can participate.

The Fruitless Search for Political Consensus

When Edward Heath suspended the Stormont regime it was not intended that direct rule from London should be anything more than a temporary expedient. The strategy of the British Government was to 'take the border out of politics', by providing for a separate and specific vote on whether Northern Ireland was to remain part of the United Kingdom or to join the Republic, and then to re-establish a system of regional government in which representatives of the whole community could share in power and influence. The first Border Poll was held in March 1973, and a new Northern Ireland Constitution Act was enacted a few months later. This provided for the election of a single-chamber Assembly and the appointment of an Executive of Ministers drawn from the membership of the Assembly on the condition that the Executive would be likely to be 'widely accepted throughout the community' and would form the basis for 'government by consent' (s. 2). The Act also made specific provision to invalidate any discriminatory legislation or executive action (ss. 17–19).

At first things went relatively well. Following the elections to the Assembly in 1973 Willie Whitelaw, the new Secretary of State for Northern Ireland, was able to secure the agreement of the leaders of most of the major parties – the Unionists representing the main stream of Protestant voters, the SDLP representing the main stream of Catholic voters, and the cross-communal Alliance and Northern Ireland Labour Parties – to the formation of a 'power-sharing' Executive. The SDLP, however, made it a condition of its participation that there would be a meaningful 'Irish dimension' to the new arrangements. It was to negotiate this that the Sunningdale summit conference was called late in 1973. In addition to the historic parallel declaration on the status of Northern Ireland discussed above, it was agreed between the two Governments and

71

the Northern Ireland parties who had agreed to share power that a Council of Ireland, with representatives from Northern Ireland and the Republic as originally envisaged in 1920, should be established and that there should also be an all-Ireland police authority.

It was this Irish dimension that led to the downfall of the power-sharing Executive soon after it took office in January 1974. Ian Paisley and other Assembly members who had excluded themselves from White-law's conferences took advantage of the unexpected Westminster election to campaign against the Council of Ireland, which they portrayed as the first step towards unification, and won a clear majority of unionist votes. This seriously undermined the position of Brian Faulkner, the premier in the power-sharing Executive, and his Unionist Party colleagues who then sought to limit their commitment to the Council of Ireland. When large numbers of working-class Protestants joined the Ulster Workers Council (UWC) strike that brought the whole province to a halt in May 1974, the power-sharing Executive finally collapsed. There is still argument about whether the new Labour Government in Britain could have saved the Executive by acting more positively to prevent intimidation and to guarantee fuel and power supplies during the UWC strike.[8] But it must not be forgotten that it was disagreement over the nature and extent of the Irish dimension that precipitated the collapse.

Since 1974 there have been repeated attempts by successive Secretaries of State to secure a new agreement among politicians in Northern Ireland on some kind of devolved administration in which representatives of both communities can share power. All have failed. Merlyn Rees established the Northern Ireland Convention in 1974. It failed to reach agreement. Humphrey Atkins held a series of abortive discussions in 1979 and 1980. Jim Prior re-established the Northern Ireland Assembly in 1982 with a view to setting in motion a process of 'rolling devolution' under which individual powers may be devolved if and when the Westminster Parliament is satisfied that such an order is likely to command widespread acceptance throughout the community (Northern Ireland Act 1982, s. 2(2)). Though the Assembly is still sitting and carrying out its role of scrutinizing the processes of government, any prospect of even starting the process of devolution on non-contentious matters has been thwarted by the boycott of both the SDLP and Sinn Féin. On each successive occasion the unionist parties have refused to share any executive power with 'republicans' and the nationalist parties have refused to enter into any governmental structure that does not contain a substantial Irish dimension.

It is tempting to blame the current generation of Ulster politicians for this persistent refusal to be reasonable. But it is important before doing so to understand precisely what it is they are being asked to do. The essence of a power-sharing executive or cabinet is that representatives of all major parties – whether on an ad hoc basis, as provided for under current British statutes, or under a system of proportional representation in the Government, as favoured by the SDLP and some parties in the Republic – should be expected to shelve any difference in their basic political objectives and agree on a common programme. What is more, they would be expected to agree on everything all the time, since the ordinary principle of majority rule within the executive or cabinet could not be applied and since there would be no other way of resolving differences. The refusal even of a relatively small party to co-operate on any issue could thus bring down the Government. It is not particularly surprising in this light that Ulster politicians who are deeply divided on very many basic issues should find it difficult to agree on a system of this kind. Those in Britain and the Republic who favour power-sharing in Northern Ireland need only consider what their reaction would be to the imposition of power-sharing in London or Dublin to see the difficulties. It is not insignificant that the Forum Report has not proposed power-sharing as a means of meeting the assumed desire of northern Protestants to share in the government of a new all-Ireland state.

It is also tempting to look forward to a change in voting patterns among the Northern Ireland electorate and the emergence of a new set of less intransigent political leaders. That is unfortunately unrealistic. Voting patterns in Northern Ireland have long been remarkably consistent, as would be expected in a stable, though divided, society (see Table 4). About 60 per cent of the electorate regularly vote for straightforward unionist parties. Between 25 and 30 per cent regularly vote for nationalist parties. In between these is a body of some 10 to 15 per cent of liberal unionists and Catholics who are prepared to support a compromise. The parties that have won the votes of these three sectors have varied over the years. The rock-solid vote of the old Unionist Party is now divided roughly equally between the Official Unionist Party and Ian Paisley's Democratic Unionist Party. The nationalist vote is divided between the SDLP and Provisional Sinn Féin, which has mobilized many of the more traditional republicans who have tended in the recent past to abstain from voting altogether. As a result of these twin struggles for supremacy in the unionist and nationalist communities the middle ground has appeared to shrink to a mere 10 per cent vote for the Alliance and Workers parties. Even if it is assumed that in different circumstances the centre would capture its full potential of around 15 per cent, however, this would not be sufficient to give it an effective and lasting balance of power between the two communal blocks. It is hard to avoid the conclusion that the search for political compromise in Northern Ireland is likely to prove fruitless for the foreseeable future and that some method other than power-sharing by consensus must be found of involving both communities in the system of government. Some of the possibilities will be explored in the next chapter.

Table 4

Communal voting strengths in Northern Ireland 1973–83

The proportion of votes or first-preference votes obtained by unionist parties, nationalist parties and the centre in recent elections has been remarkably stable despite fluctuations in the performance of particular parties; the increase in the Republican/Sinn Féin vote is largely due to their abandonment of abstention from 1979.

	Assembly election 1973 (%)	Convention election 1975 (%)	General election 1979 (%)	Assembly election 1982 (%)	General election 1983 (%)
Democratic Unionists (DUP)	11	15	10	23	20
Official Unionists	29	26	37	30	34
Other unionist parties	22	22	12	6	3
Unionist Block	62	63	59	59	57
Alliance Party	9	10	12	9	8
NI Labour/Workers Party	3	1	1	3	4
Centre Block	12	11	13	12	12
Social Democratic and Labour (SDLP)	22	24	20	19	18
Republican/Sinn Féin	3	2	8	10	13
Nationalist Block	25	26	28	29	31

Continuing Discrimination?

Direct rule from London has proved rather more successful on matters of day-to-day administration than on security and political development. Successive opinion polls in Northern Ireland have indicated that continuing direct rule is the most generally acceptable form of government to both communities, even though it is not the preferred option of either. Considerable progress has been made in eliminating the worst housing conditions through the government-controlled Northern Ireland Housing Executive, which was established in 1972, and in the fair administration of education and health services through government-appointed Area Boards. There have, of course, been continuing complaints about the undemocratic nature of these bodies and about the effect of successive public expenditure cuts on the level of services, though in housing at least Northern Ireland has fared considerably better than other deprived areas within the United Kingdom. But allegations of communal discrimination in these spheres are now rare and when they are made are not generally given much credence in either community.

The same cannot be said about the much more important issue of discrimination in employment. Despite the creation, since 1969, of a wide range of agencies to monitor and deal with complaints of communal discrimination of all kinds[9] – the Parliamentary Commissioner in respect of central government functions, the Commissioner for Complaints in respect of local government and other public services within Northern Ireland and the Fair Employment Agency in respect of most forms of employment in both public and private sectors – very little progress has been made in securing equality of employment between the two communities in more than a decade of even-handed direct rule from London. The figure for unemployment among Catholics is still roughly double that among Protestants. The total unemployment rate among those who declared themselves as Catholics in 1981 was 33 per cent for males and 17 per cent for females, compared with figures of 15 per cent and 11 per cent for the rest of the population. If similar patterns are assumed to apply to the substantial proportion of people who refused to disclose their religion (18.5 per cent), the differentiation between the two communities would be even more striking. In areas of high Catholic density, notably West Belfast, Strabane and Derry, the figures are even worse, with male unemployment rates of more than 50 per cent in some wards.[10]

All kinds of explanations may be produced for these figures. Successive reports from the Fair Employment Agency on specific sectors and employers have emphasized not only the difficulty in altering established patterns of employment over a short period of time, particularly in a period of economic decline when there is little new recruitment, but also the reluctance of Catholics to venture out of 'safe' areas into jobs in traditionally loyalist firms, notably in the engineering industry.[11] Although the Agency has powers to require employers to adopt better recruitment practices, it has no powers to prescribe targets or quotas, and publicity and persuasion have not always been sufficient to induce employers and unions to take positive action to alter the balance of the labour force. The impact of Irish-American pressure groups on Shorts, the major aircraft manufacturer in Belfast, when a major US contract was being negotiated proved a good deal more effective in increasing the number of Catholics employed. The differing educational patterns within the two communities also contribute to the problem. Rather more Protestants choose to study scientific and technical subjects, while rather more Catholics choose arts subjects, which restrict their employment opportunities and aspirations.[12] And there are some major areas of employment, notably the security forces, from which Catholics exclude themselves. The resulting differences in qualifications and in actual applications for jobs means that it is often hard to establish that there has been any deliberate discrimination on the part of employers.

None of this detracts from the fact that there are still very significant differences in the employment levels in the two communities. These in their turn have a significant impact on general levels of prosperity. Though poverty and deprivation have long been a feature of working-class areas for both Protestants and Catholics, both are undoubtedly concentrated in the Catholic community, which has also experienced the worst effects of fifteen years of disorder and terrorist activity and of oppressive action by the security forces. It is a strange fact that many more bombs have been planted by the IRA in predominantly Catholic towns, like Newry, Strabane and Derry, than in equivalent Protestant towns and that even in Belfast the bombers rarely stray far from the areas in which their own community lives and works. As a result the physical environment in predominantly Catholic areas is substantially worse than in equivalent Protestant areas.

Alienation among Catholics

All these factors – abuses in the security field and in the operation of emergency powers, the failure of the British Government to make any progress in securing an effective voice for Catholics in the government of Northern Ireland and the continuing difference in levels of unemployment and deprivation in the two communities – have contributed to a deepening sense of alienation among many Catholics both from Britain and from the majority community. The resulting despair at the prospect of resolving these problems within either a British or a purely Northern Ireland context has been an important factor in the growth of support for Provisional Sinn Féin and in demands for a more radical approach to the whole Northern Ireland problem than has yet been envisaged by the British Government. This sense of increasing alienation among Catholics was one of the principal reasons for the establishment of the New Ireland Forum and has given renewed impetus to the current search for a new framework for the settlement of the Northern Ireland problem of the kind discussed in the chapters that follow. Each of the main dimensions will be dealt with in turn: the internal Northern Ireland dimension, the North–South dimension, the security dimension and the British–Irish dimension.

6
The Internal Dimension: New Structures Within Northern Ireland

The starting point of any settlement of the Northern Ireland problem must be the full recognition of the right of a majority of the people in Northern Ireland to determine which state it is to form part of. That right should be agreed in a new Anglo-Irish treaty registered at the United Nations and incorporated in the constitutions both of Northern Ireland and of the Republic, as set out in Chapter 3. Within that framework, however, the identities and interests of both communities must be granted full and equal recognition. In particular, the minority nationalist community must be entitled to express its Irish identity in any way that does not conflict with the right of the majority community to decide to remain part of the United Kingdom. And if at any time in the future a majority of the people in Northern Ireland should vote for unification with the Republic, the new unionist minority would be entitled to enjoy corresponding rights within any new unitary Irish state.

The importance of beginning with this seemingly formalistic and over-elaborate statement of the obvious is to remove fears in both communities that any concession to the other will jeopardize its own future. Unionists have long feared that any recognition of the Irish identity of the minority in Northern Ireland will be seen merely as a stepping stone to ultimate unification. Nationalists fear that full recognition of the legitimacy of partition will be used to deny their true Irish identity and their legitimate aspiration to unification. It is only when the fundamentals have been settled beyond any legitimate future challenge that progress can be made in giving practical recognition to the individual and communal rights of both the majority and minority communities and in establishing a system of government in which both can share.

The Right to be Irish

The failure by the British and by southern nationalists alike to give any serious consideration to the position of the northern minority was perhaps the most serious defect in the original partition settlement. They were not consulted in any way on the terms of the settlement, nor as to how their identity and interests within Northern Ireland should be protected. In any new settlement that failure must be remedied both by removing the various measures adopted during the Stormont regime with a view to discouraging any assertion of Irishness by the minority and by providing more positive recognition of their Irish identity and aspirations.[1]

To begin with, there should be a formal recognition of the right of any citizen of Northern Ireland to assert and exercise the entitlement of Irish citizenship that is already accorded to him or her under the Irish Constitution and the Irish Nationality Act 1956 without thereby losing any rights within Northern Ireland. That would involve the immediate repeal of the provisions of the Electoral Law Act (Northern Ireland) 1962 that disqualified from standing for election or voting in local elections in Northern Ireland, both for the Stormont Parliament and for local councils, all citizens of the Irish Republic not already on the voting register in 1962. This was designed to protect slender Unionist Party majorities in border areas and currently disqualifies about 4,000 voters in local council and Assembly elections but not elections to the Westminster Parliament. Unionist fears about an influx of nationalist voters from across the border in respect of a Border Poll could, if necessary, be met by a specific residence requirement.

Secondly, the bar on joint membership of the British Parliament or the Northern Ireland Assembly and the Oireachtas, the Parliament of the Republic, under the House of Commons Disqualification Act 1975 and the Northern Ireland Assembly Act 1973, should be removed. This caused considerable resentment among nationalists in Northern Ireland following the appointment of Seamus Mallon, deputy leader of the SDLP, to the Irish Senate in 1982. Dual membership is widely accepted and practised within the European Community. There is absolutely no reason why it should not be accepted on a reciprocal basis within Britain and Ireland.

On a rather different level the provisions of the Flags and Emblems (Display) Act (Northern Ireland) 1954 that were intended to discourage (though they do not actually prohibit) the display of the Irish tricolour flag must also be repealed. This would mean that the same criterion – the likelihood of public disorder – would apply to the display of all flags and emblems, including the Union Jack, which is often displayed in a sectarian context by loyalists.

The right of the minority to be Irish could be recognized in other more positive ways. Arrangements could be made for the opening of Irish consular offices in Belfast and Derry and other centres as appropriate, so that those in Northern Ireland who wish to travel with Irish passports, and to rely on their Irish citizenship in other ways, may do so with minimum inconvenience. It would also be possible, if northern nationalists wished and the Republic agreed, to make provision for the election of representatives to the Oireachtas from within Northern Ireland. It is probable that the parties in the Republic would prefer the election of a small number of members only to Seanad Éireann, the upper chamber in the Irish Parliament, which would avoid upsetting the delicate balance of power in the lower chamber, Dáil Éireann. It must be remembered that in any system of proportional representation unionists would be in a position to elect more representatives than nationalists, if they chose to exercise their votes. Representatives from Northern Ireland might also be involved in any joint parliamentary committee on Northern Ireland affairs. Accepting the right of the Republic to make provisions of this kind would provide some practical recognition of the fact that nationalists in Northern Ireland were excluded from the Irish Republic against their will.

Individual and Communal Rights

It is arguable that the rights of the nationalist or Catholic minority in respect of other matters, such as education and employment, are already protected against discriminatory legislation or administrative practice under the Northern Ireland Constitution Act 1973 and the European Convention on Human Rights and Fundamental Freedoms. The first of these makes unlawful any legislation or other action by a public authority that discriminates against any person or class of persons on the ground of religious belief or political opinion (ss. 17–19). But the courts in Britain and Northern Ireland are notoriously reluctant to interfere with legislative or executive action, especially where any question of national security is involved, and might not in any case be acceptable as guarantors for nationalists. The European Convention makes special provision for the enjoyment of all the fundamental rights and freedoms that it protects 'without discrimination on any ground such as sex, race, colour, language, religion, political or other opinion, national or social origin, *association with a national minority*, property, birth or other status' (Art. 14: emphasis supplied). Both the United Kingdom and the Republic are signatories of the European Convention and both have had to adjust their internal legislation and administrative practices in response to proceedings at the European Commission and the European Court at Strasbourg. But none of the rights covered by the Convention is absolutely guaranteed. Many are protected subject to 'such limitations as are prescribed by law and are necessary in a democratic society in the interests of public safety, for the protection of public order, health or morals, or for the protection of the rights and freedoms of others'. And there is some doubt as to the extent to which communal as opposed to individual rights are covered. For example, an attempt by French-speaking parents in Belgium to rely on the (admittedly limited) provisions of the first Protocol of the Convention in respect of education was unsuccessful: it was held that those who lived in an area officially designated as Flemish-speaking had no right to insist that their children be educated in French.[2] The provisions of Article 27 of the United Nations International Covenant on Civil and Political Rights are rather more specific in respect of communal minorities:

> In those states in which ethnic, religious or linguistic minorities exist, persons belonging to such minorities shall not be denied the right, in community with the other members of their group, to enjoy their own culture, to profess and practise their own religion, or to use their own language.

This Covenant has been ratified by the United Kingdom, though not by the Republic. Its effectiveness would be greatly enhanced if, in addition to immediate ratification by the Republic, both states were to ratify the optional protocol that allows complaints of non-compliance to be made by individuals to the Human Rights Committee. Both states would then be fully committed to uniform international standards for the protection of minorities and of human rights in general.

It may also be appropriate for additional protection for communal and group rights within Northern Ireland to be spelled out. This would allow specific provisions of particular relevance to the two communities in Northern Ireland in respect of such matters as cultural expression, education and economic equality to be negotiated and guaranteed by both Britain and Ireland on a bilateral basis.

In the cultural field specific provision might be made to guarantee the right of nationalists to use the Irish language and Irish symbols, as in Wales under the Welsh Language Act 1967. As in Wales, this might grant a right to use Irish names and the Irish language in dealings with governmental authorities. The current requirement under the Public Health and Local Government (Miscellaneous Provisions) Act (Northern Ireland)

1949 that all street names must be in English was deliberately introduced to prevent any such assertion of Irishness and is offensive to many members of the minority community. It should be replaced by a provision entitling the residents of a district, estate or street to decide, by an appropriate majority, to have street names and traffic signs in the Irish language as well as in English. This approach might be developed to include the choice of name for geographic places, subject to appropriate controls to prevent confusing or totally unsuitable names. The principle of reasonable local autonomy should be applied on matters of this kind – as, for instance, in the case of the choice between Derry and Londonderry. An enabling measure might be introduced to permit town polls on this and other matters, along the lines of the Welsh provisions on Sunday drinking. Provision might also be made for an appropriate proportion of TV and radio programmes in Irish or for a separate Irish-language local station.

In respect of education the current legal rules requiring Area Education and Library Boards to take account of parental wishes in making provision for schools and for the separate funding of Catholic schools are equally inadequate to reflect the range of provision that is appropriate to a divided society. What is needed is a direct and enforceable expression of the right of parents to have their children educated in schools of their choice, whether of a Protestant, Catholic, Gaelic or integrated character, subject only to a requirement of minimum numbers in a given area. The extra public expenditure on such a right must be one of the unavoidable costs of governing a region like Northern Ireland in which some parents wish to maintain their communal separation and some wish to begin to break down communal barriers. There can be no question of the *compulsory* integration of schools. But that should not exclude the *encouragement* of joint schooling by appropriate financial provision.

The protection of communal as opposed to individual rights in employment is likely to prove more difficult to achieve. But it is perhaps the most significant area of continuing differentiation or discrimination. The existing anti-discrimination measures under the Fair Employment (Northern Ireland) Act 1976 make it unlawful for an individual employer to discriminate in the selection of an employee on the grounds of religious belief or political opinion and enable the Fair Employment Agency to promote greater equality by carrying out studies of particular firms or sectors and by encouraging employers to implement appropriate action to increase equality of opportunity. Though the Agency has made some progress in eliminating overt discrimination and in creating greater public awareness of the extent of the problem (as, for instance, in its recent studies of the Northern Ireland Civil Service and the Northern Ireland Electricity

Service), it has no power to prescribe targets or to monitor a staged progression towards equality of employment as opposed to equality of opportunity. The fact that during more than ten years of direct rule so little progress has been made in eliminating the differential in employment levels indicates that stronger powers of this kind will be required to overcome the social and economic forces that help to maintain the present inequalities.

These various protections would be given greater force if they were incorporated in a general Bill of Rights for Northern Ireland covering both individual and communal rights. It is not only the nationalist minority that complains of discrimination. In some areas Protestants also experience unfair treatment, and there are other smaller minorities, such as the travelling people. Specific reference to the need for such a Bill of Rights to meet the criteria contained in the Capotorti Report to the United Nations Subcommission on the Prevention of Discrimination and the Protection of Minorities (see Chapter 3) should be incorporated in the proposed Anglo-Irish Treaty, as should appropriate provisions for the joint monitoring of performance, as suggested below.[3]

The Participation of the Minority in Government

The difficulty that the British Government has experienced in attempting to establish a system of devolved government in Northern Ireland in which representatives of both communities can participate may likewise be attributed to a lack of precision about the respective rights of majority and minority groups in a divided society. The British legal and constitutional tradition within which both Northern Ireland and the Republic evolved is to identify democracy with majority rule and to ignore the position of minorities. This may work in relatively homogeneous societies like Britain and the Republic, in which there are no fundamental differences in political objectives and in which there is a reasonable likelihood that different political parties will win sufficient electoral support to form or participate in a majority Government. It is wholly inappropriate in a divided communal society like Northern Ireland, in which one group is in a position to exercise more or less permanent domination and in which the political objectives of the two communal groups are fundamentally opposed. This is now recognized to the extent that the British Government has made it clear that power will not be devolved to Northern Ireland on a majority-rule basis. But the alternative of 'power-sharing', which successive British Governments have attempted to persuade the main parties in Northern

Ireland to accept, is equally impractical, as has been shown above. It does not provide any mechanism for resolving the differences of opinion that are bound to arise within a cabinet or executive, and it encourages brinkmanship in that the ultimate decision about whether a Government commands widespread acceptance has been left to the discretion of either the Secretary of State (as under the Northern Ireland Constitution Act 1973) or of the British Parliament (as under the current provisions for rolling devolution under the Northern Ireland Act 1982).

Since the arrangements for internal government within Northern Ireland are clearly crucial to any lasting settlement, some more realistic system than the highly discretionary provisions for 'power-sharing' is clearly required. The most practical approach would be to provide that both legislation and other governmental decisions needing a formal administrative order should require a weighted majority of votes in any regional assembly or parliament in respect of matters of particular communal concern, such as education, local government, policing and security, the location of major industrial developments and all matters of an electoral or constitutional nature. It would not be necessary to require the same weighted majority for all these matters. A 60 per cent vote might be thought sufficient for some decisions, while other more fundamental and constitutional matters might require a 75 per cent vote. The principle that different types of decision require different majorities is well-established in the constitutions of other countries. It is also well-established in both British and Irish company law as the primary mechanism for the protection of minority shareholders. A structure of this kind would provide a workable means of involving representatives of all parties in the process of government without requiring the unrealistic degree of consensus on all matters that is assumed in the 'power-sharing' model. It could readily be combined with a system of scrutiny committees with wide powers to questions Ministers and officials and with chairmen and members drawn from all parties in such a way as to counteract the power of the governing majority to prevent the full investigation of disputed issues. The experience of the existing Northern Ireland Assembly in scrutiny committees of this kind is generally agreed to have been valuable, and there is no substantial disagreement with the concept among the major Catholic parties despite their abstention from the Assembly.

Such a structure for government would establish workable parameters for the devolution of particular powers to a new Northern Ireland assembly or parliament as and when agreement on the precise majority to be required for each was reached. It would not rule out the creation of a voluntary, broad-based coalition of all or most parties for an initial period of reconstruction, as has been proposed from time to time. It could also be integrated without conflict with a parliamentary tier of the Anglo-Irish Intergovernmental Council, as discussed below. Those powers and functions that were reserved for the Westminster Parliament or for the parliamentary tier would be dealt with in London or between London and Dublin. Those that had been devolved to a Northern Ireland assembly would be dealt with in Belfast, or between Belfast and Dublin in so far as agreement was reached on reciprocal cross-border links.

7
The Role of the Republic

The claim by the Republic of Ireland to have a say in any comprehensive settlement of the Northern Ireland conflict is not one that has been pressed until recently. Irish policy on Northern Ireland has been as ad hoc as British. The situation there was ignored over the years by the people of the Republic and their Governments in much the same way that it was by the people of Britain and their Governments. It was the crisis precipitated by the civil rights movement in the 1960s and the 1970s that galvanized the British first to take action and ultimately to take over the running of the province. Active Irish Government concern dates from the same events. After decades of avoiding the need even to think about the problem both states are now being forced to reassess their policies, not least by coming to terms with the extent to which those policies have contributed to the impasse in Northern Ireland. In the Republic's case this led to the establishment of the New Ireland Forum, and to the more general questioning of traditional positions on Northern Ireland that is still going on.

The traditional stance of Irish nationalists in the Republic has been that the partition of the island was the work of the British and that it is their responsibility to remove it. This has imbued official thinking and is also to be found in parts of the Forum Report. It follows from this view that there is nothing for the Republic to do except to remind Britain of its responsibility, occasionally or frequently dependent on whether a more or less republican Government is in power. Meanwhile the unionists have been ignored in case any dealings with them might be used to legitimate their position. It has been equally part of Irish policy, however, that no support is to be extended to efforts to end partition by violent means. Northern unionists have rarely acknowledged the significance of the single-minded determination of successive Governments in the Republic to suppress the I R A in its own territory, often at considerable cost to civil liberties and internal peace. It remains a fact that the present troubles bear more heavily on the Irish economy than on the British and that Irish Governments have never wavered in their rejection of IRA violence.

The Need for Pluralism

The advantages of a policy of 'verbal republicanism' are obvious. The Republic could blame Britain for the failure to achieve the national goal of a united Ireland while directing its own energies, and those of its people, towards developing and strengthening the twenty-six-county state at home and abroad. The policy was pursued with considerable success. The Republic, which was the first new nation of this century to break away from the control of an imperial power, has long since achieved full sovereign status equal to that of the other states of the world.

The disadvantages were initially less obvious but have become more so. In the first place, the combination of the comfortable assumption that the Republic need do nothing to bring about a united Ireland and of the pursuit of the goal of asserting independence from Britain made the likelihood of achieving a united Ireland remote and the need to come to terms with that fact now the more traumatic. In the second place, the easy but false assumption that nothing done within the Republic could have any bearing on North–South relations and eventual unity resulted in an uncritical lack of resistance on the part of the state to pressure from Catholics, both lay and clerical, who were determined to create a Catholic state in the Republic. Equally, the failure to come to terms with the existence of a British minority in Ireland encouraged the delusion that 'Irish Ireland' policies pursued in the Republic, including the compulsory use of Gaelic in its educational system and the identification of Irish nationality with Catholicism in its officially sponsored culture, would require no modification if unification of the island were ever actually to be achieved. Finally, the failure to consider the realities of Northern Ireland and the fixation on partition as the sole injustice prevented successive Irish Governments from exercising the influence that they might have had on behalf of the national minority within Northern Ireland.

There are signs that these home truths are finding a response, not least as a result of the impact that the northern conflict has had on the economy and politics in the Republic. The beginnings of change can be traced to 1965 and the meetings between Sean Lemass, the pragmatic Taoiseach (Head of the Government) of the Republic, and Terence O'Neill, the reforming Prime Minister of Northern Ireland. As subsequent history has shown, those symbolic meetings – the first between the leaders of the

Republic and Northern Ireland since the 1920s – proved a false, or at least premature, beginning in easing North–South tensions through a policy of mutual accommodation and recognition.

There have been other developments. As early as 1972 the electorate voted to remove from the Constitution what had become an embarrassing formulation recognizing the special position of the Roman Catholic Church. The recent 'victory' of the coalition Government over the reform of the law on contraception, despite the strident opposition of the Catholic hierarchy, reflects an increasing recognition that the majority in the Republic must demonstrate, in advance of any possible unification, that it is willing to embrace the pluralist values and attitudes on which so much emphasis is placed in the Forum Report. Further action will have to be taken. The constitutional prohibition on divorce, which the Protestant Churches have consistently argued is a denial of a basic civil right, will have to be removed, a change now supported by a majority of the population. Action will also be required in other areas of family law. Discrimination against illegitimate children must be countered, and the hypocritical constitutional provision on abortion, the ambiguous terms of which force even women whose life may be at risk to seek a termination of their pregnancies in Britain, must be repealed. Progress on these and other matters would best be achieved by establishing a broadly based commission with the task of undertaking a thorough survey of the Constitution and other relevant laws with a view to implementing the Forum's commitment to pluralism and tolerance.

The Constitutional Claim

A matter of even greater symbolic concern to northern unionists is the claim enshrined in Articles 2 and 3 of the Irish Constitution (see Chapter 3). Unionist objections to these clauses have too readily been ignored by successive Governments in the Republic. It is essential, if the legitimacy of the unionist position is to be fully recognized and the commitment to the principle that unification must be achieved only by consent is to be fully implemented, that these articles be amended to replace the existing ambiguous claims with a clear statement of aspiration. It must not be forgotten that in 1967 an all-party committee on the Irish Constitution agreed upon a reformulation of Article 3 to make clear that a united Ireland was an aspiration to be achieved through agreement and in peace.[1] In any event, before and since that date the claim to jurisdiction over Northern Ireland has been completely ignored by the Republic in its international relations, including its bilateral relations with Britain. The issue of

Northern Ireland was not raised when the Republic joined the United Nations in 1955. Nor did the Republic object, when on joining the European Community in 1973, Northern Ireland also joined as part of the United Kingdom. If the Republic is to play its necessary part in any settlement, the constitutional rhetoric must at last be modified to acknowledge present realities, by the actual adoption of the formulation proposed in 1967 in respect of Article 3 and by an appropriate amendment of Article 2, so that the constitutional status of Northern Ireland is expressed in the same terms in the Republic's Constitution and in British law, as proposed in Chapter 3.

North–South Relations

If history has dictated a special relationship between Britain and Ireland, such a relationship is even more pronounced between the Republic and Northern Ireland. Apart from the fact that they share a single island, there is the fact that there are half a million or more nationalists in Northern Ireland. Decades of non-co-operation and hostility between the two Governments have clearly affected, but not eliminated, the natural bonds on other levels. Apart from family ties, numerous religious, cultural, educational, sporting and other social institutions link people on each side of the border. Direct economic co-operation is as yet minimal. But some significant steps have been taken at governmental and private levels in the last few years.[2] The failure of the British Government to proceed with the agreement to supply natural gas from the Kinsale field to Northern Ireland will, it is to be hoped, be only a temporary setback to rational economic co-operation between the two parts of Ireland. There are many spheres in industry, agriculture and education in which cross-border co-operation would be beneficial to both sides. The European Community has already sponsored a number of cross-border development studies, notably in the counties of Londonderry and Donegal and Cavan, Leitrim and Fermanagh. There are also obvious ways in which expensive agricultural and technical services can be shared in remoter border areas. A recent study of further education in the north-west has likewise pointed to the mutual benefits that would result from the co-ordination of courses in the various colleges in Donegal, Letterkenny and Derry and in the Magee campus of the University of Ulster and from encouraging local students to move freely across the border without facing unnecessary bureaucratic and financial problems.[3]

There is also scope for the development of joint cross-border agencies on a reciprocal basis for specified purposes. As already explained, the exercise of joint authority of this kind, as opposed to the exercise of authority by the Republic over Northern Ireland on a unilateral basis, is not inherently objectionable to unionists, since it recognizes the equal legitimacy of both sides. The agreement between Northern Ireland and the Republic in 1952 to establish a joint Foyle Fisheries Commission with power to operate on both sides of the border is a useful model, not least because the Commission has operated without any formal or practical difficulties until the present. The most obvious spheres in which new joint agencies of this kind might be established are tourism and industrial development. In both spheres there are at present only informal links, and there would be clear benefits from the integration of promotional activity abroad. In the field of tourism joint promotions would emphasize the new peaceful relationship between the two parts of Ireland and would help to remove the ill-effects of adverse publicity about the 'troubles' over the years. In industrial promotion the creation of a new joint agency would help to remove the risk of damaging competition between the two parts of Ireland in the search for new industrial projects, though in return some prior agreement about the balanced location of new projects would be necessary. In all such ventures support and grant aid from the European Community would undoubtedly be available.

It would be desirable for North–South links of this kind to be developed on a mutual basis by the Government of the Republic and whatever form of devolved government is established in Northern Ireland. But it must be remembered that the scope for North–South co-operation on many issues is limited by rules and regulations applied on a United Kingdom basis or imposed by the European Commission. And in most spheres there is much greater direct dealing between Northern Ireland and Britain and between the Republic and Britain than between Northern Ireland and the Republic – as, for example, in respect of almost all forms of trade and of the movement of students. To this extent the arrangements for relationships between Britain and the Republic, discussed in Chapter 9, are as significant to North–South relations as direct relationships between Belfast and Dublin. The immediate need for the development of cross-border co-operation and for reciprocal arrangements and agencies in the security sphere is likewise the responsibility of the two sovereign Governments. Since security is perhaps the most pressing and sensitive of all the possible areas of co-operation, it is discussed separately in the next chapter.

8
Security: Defending a Settlement

There is good reason to believe that violence and terrorism will gradually decline if a political settlement is reached over Northern Ireland. But they will not cease immediately. There is a long tradition of paramilitary action in all parts of Ireland, and extreme factions on both sides must be expected to do their best to wreck any prospective agreement. And in any event, as has been seen, the activities of the security forces have always been a significant part of the problem.

There are sharply divided views, both within Northern Ireland and between Northern Ireland and the Republic, about how security should be handled. Unionists typically insist that measures to deal with terrorism should be completely divorced from wider political issues and have repeatedly demanded tougher action against the IRA. Many blame the Republic for providing a safe haven for cross-border terrorist operations. And large numbers are prepared to join in the battle, whether by enlisting in the security forces, by supporting the mobilization of a doubtfully legal 'third force' or by engaging in clearly unlawful paramilitary activities. Nationalists on both sides of the border typically see the continuing violence as a symptom of political failure and insist on political changes as a prelude to, or even as a substitute for, action to deal with terrorism.[1] Within Northern Ireland many Catholics are as critical of the past and current policies of the British Army, the RUC and the UDR as of the IRA and other paramilitaries. Most are unwilling to join the security forces within Northern Ireland under the present regime.

Generally acceptable and workable legal and security arrangements are thus an essential element in any overall settlement. As with other aspects of the Northern Ireland problem, these must involve not only action within the province but also appropriate cross-border arrangements. Within Northern Ireland some provision must be made to ensure that the police and other security forces are more representative and to

91

provide better safeguards against abuses of emergency laws. Between Northern Ireland and the Republic provision must be made to reduce the friction caused by cross-border terrorist operations and by the differing approaches to extradition of Britain and the Republic. At both levels any new measures must meet two demanding tests: they must inspire the confidence of both communities in Northern Ireland, and they must be shown to be necessary for the fair and effective administration of justice and not to be designed (or open to interpretation) as part of a concealed movement towards either unification or the renewed domination of one community by the other.

An Acceptable Police Force for Northern Ireland

There can be no immediate solution to the problem of making the existing security forces in Northern Ireland more acceptable to the minority. There would be a serious risk in attempting to replace the British Army by an international peacekeeping force, since that would signal to all sides that the constitutional status of Northern Ireland as part of the United Kingdom was in doubt. Nor would it be either practicable or politically acceptable to attempt to stand down the RUC and to create an entirely new police force, whether within Northern Ireland or on an all-Ireland basis. Given the immediate need for trained personnel, any such force would in practice have to rely heavily on existing RUC personnel. It would certainly be wholly unacceptable to unionists to be policed by members of the Garda Siochána, the police service in the Republic, except on a reciprocal basis of the kind discussed below. There would be little point in replacing one 'unacceptable' police force by another. The suggestion that the huge current imbalance in Protestant and Catholic membership of the RUC could be remedied by establishing separate local police forces in Catholic areas is initially attractive but would in practice be likely to make matters worse. It would establish what would in effect be rival local forces and would be likely to increase rather than diminish the problem faced by the RUC in gaining free access and establishing its credibility throughout the province. It might also increase rather than diminish the risk of links with or infiltration by paramilitaries on either side.

There is, in fact, no practicable alternative, within the framework of a settlement along the lines proposed above, to relying on the RUC as a unitary, non-sectarian police force for the whole of Northern Ireland. That does not mean that nothing can be done to make the RUC more acceptable to the minority community.

To begin with, the RUC could be made more effectively accountable to representatives of both communities by reconstituting a more directly representative and powerful Northern Ireland Police Authority and establishing a network of local police liaison committees with statutory powers of consultation and scrutiny on issues of local concern. It would seem appropriate for about one-third of the members of both the central authority and the local committees to be drawn from elected members of the Northern Ireland Assembly and District Councils and for the remainder to be appointed after consultation with representative regional and local bodies. It would also be desirable to encourage links of the type discussed below for nominees to be appointed on a reciprocal basis from equivalent bodies in Britain and the Republic, where the formation of a police authority is currently under consideration. In addition to its established functions of making senior appointments and controlling finance and equipment, the central authority should be given responsibility for drawing up and monitoring operational guidelines on such emotive communal matters as the routeing of marches and demonstrations. It should also be given more effective powers to order wide-ranging inquiries into matters of general public concern. Local liaison committees should be given specific duties in respect of the actual routes for marches and demonstrations and similar powers in respect of inquiries into matters of local concern. On all these matters the central authority and local committees should be encouraged to act by broad consensus through appropriate rules of procedure with a view to establishing the principle that it is the duty of the police to give equal recognition to all sections of the community rather than merely to comply with the wishes of the majority in any area.

Greater confidence in the RUC and a higher level of recruitment among members of the minority community could also be encouraged by developing mutual links between the RUC and the Garda Síochána similar to those that already exist between the RUC and the police in Britain. It should be standard practice for both bodies to advertise and recruit in all parts of Ireland – which would give some positive meaning to the principle of free movement of labour within the European Community. Training facilities in certain areas might be shared, and joint studies on law enforcement in appropriate spheres, such as drug trafficking and smuggling, should be encouraged. It should be accepted that when an internal inquiry is ordered by the Chief Constable on any matter of sufficient seriousness to merit the involvement of a senior officer from another force, senior officers from the Garda Síochána might be called on as well as senior officers from Britain. The overall objective would be to create the same relationship between the RUC and the Garda Síochána, on a fully reciprocal basis, as between the RUC and the police in Britain so as to give equal recognition to the rights and loyalties of both communities.

If agreement on new arrangements along these lines were linked with a substantial increase in the authorized establishment of the RUC, a sustained drive to recruit more members of the Catholic community would then be possible. This would in turn permit an equivalent and gradual reduction in the role and the numbers of the UDR, which has always been a controversial force. Many of its members, both in and out of uniform, have been murdered by the IRA. And the involvement of some UDR soldiers in retaliatory sectarian murders and other such incidents has made it the least acceptable wing of the security forces in the eyes of many Catholics. There have been repeated calls for its disbandment. Since that would clearly be unacceptable to most unionists and might well result in an increase in loyalist paramilitary activity, it would be more practical to wind down the level of UDR activity as an expanded RUC took over more security functions. Full-time UDR soldiers could be offered alternative employment in the regular British Army if they so wished. The ultimate objective should be to return to policing arrangements recognized as normal and desirable in both states by dispensing with any other military back-up to a cross-communal unarmed police than would be provided by a normal army garrison and part-time territorial reserve.

Emergency Powers and Public Order

The acceptance of the RUC as an impartial cross-communal force would be further assisted by some long overdue reforms in the ordinary law of public order and by a substantial reduction in the ambit of emergency powers.

The problem over public order is that some remnants of the old-style Unionist regime still encourage the RUC to adopt an apparently sectarian approach to marches and demonstrations. The Flags and Emblems (Display) Act (Northern Ireland) 1954, as has been seen, permits the display of the Union Jack regardless of any threat to public order that the flag may represent in a nationalist area, while it prohibits the display of the Irish tricolour – or any other flag – that creates a similar threat. This has led, over the years, to a series of quite unnecessary confrontations when the RUC have attempted to remove tricolours that loyalists have complained about. It should be repealed immediately. Similarly the proviso to the Public Order Act that exempts 'traditional' parades from the obligation to obtain RUC clearance over their route has been used over the years by the Orange Order and other loyalists to insist on police protection for blatantly sectarian marches through Catholic areas, as in the notorious Obins Street march in Portadown on the Twelfth of July each year.[2] That too must be repealed and replaced by a new set of statutory guidelines for the routeing or banning of marches, which could then be implemented in consultation with local police liaison committees. The objective should be to ensure that the organizers of marches and demonstrations on either side sit down together to discuss mutually acceptable routes and practices, so that the expression of historical and cultural roots in both communities can become a matter of mutual respect rather than periodic confrontation.

While the current level of terrorist activity persists the continuation of some emergency powers and procedures, both in Northern Ireland and in the Republic, is probably unavoidable. But the authorities have always underestimated the counter-productive effects of security laws and practices that do not command the general respect of both communities. The recent *Review of the Northern Ireland (Emergency Provisions) Act 1978* by Sir George Baker is just the latest example of a whole series of official British inquiries that have misjudged the balance between 'effective security' and communal confidence in the administration of justice.[3] If terrorist offences are to be fairly but effectively investigated and fairly tried in the eyes of both communities, much more significant changes in the system than Baker has proposed will be required.

To begin with, the powers of arrest and interrogation must be reformulated to ensure that they are used only where there is a reasonable suspicion that a particular person has been involved in serious criminal activity and not, as is still the case, for the purposes of general intelligence-gathering in suspect areas. Many of the safeguards in the new British Police and Criminal Evidence Act 1984, notably a statutory code of interrogation practice, could usefully be incorporated, so that the law and procedure for dealing with paramilitary violence are kept as close as is practicable to those that apply for other serious crimes.

The system of no-jury Diplock courts should then be limited strictly to those cases in which it is shown that there is a real risk of the intimidation of jurors. The other justification for the suspension of jury trial – the risk of perverse verdicts by largely Protestant juries in the early 1970s – should be controlled by stricter rules on jury selection. In the remaining cases in which a no-jury trial is shown to be necessary, lay assessors representative of both communities or an additional judge from another jurisdiction, as suggested below, should be required. And there should be a formal requirement that the evidence of supergrasses should be corroborated before anyone can be convicted on it.

There is also an urgent need for a better means of dealing with the alleged misuse of lethal force by members of the security forces in so-called 'shoot-to-kill' cases. Both in Northern Ireland and in the Republic the principle that the deliberate use of lethal force is justifiable only in defence of life should be incorporated in the law. And a new offence of the reckless use of lethal force by members of the security forces and others in lawful possession of firearms should be created to replace or supplement the charge of murder that must now be laid in most 'shoot-to-kill' cases. This would help to reduce the risk that the natural sympathy of judges or jurors with soldiers and policemen who have over-reacted in difficult and dangerous circumstances will result in repeated acquittals of the kind that have recently caused so much controversy in Northern Ireland.

Finally there is an urgent need for new procedures to ensure that there is a speedy public investigation into all major disputed shootings and other controversial incidents involving the security forces. Where there has been a death, this could be met by relatively small changes in the law on coroners' inquests to require a coroner's court to hold an immediate hearing to clarify the circumstances of the shooting and to give it power to refer cases to the Director of Public Prosecutions where necessary. In other serious cases a similar procedure could be operated by a new security tribunal or ombudsman.

All these reforms are directly linked to two fundamental rules in dealing with terrorism in a divided society: that any derogation from the ordinary law must be shown to be strictly necessary to the fair and effective administration of justice, and that it must be accompanied by special safeguards to prevent abuse and maintain public confidence. They have been ignored for far too long in Northern Ireland with disastrous results.

Cross-Border Issues

Attitudes towards cross-border co-operation in dealing with terrorism in Northern Ireland are equally divided. Although only a small proportion of terrorist incidents are carried out from across the border, unionists have long complained that the Republic provides a relatively safe haven not only for those making these incursions but also for IRA training and planning and for fugitive offenders. These complaints ignore the fact that Irish prisons are bursting at the seams with convicted paramilitaries from Northern Ireland. But in respect of fugitive offenders they were until recently given some justification by the very strict application by courts in the Republic of the 'political offence' rule in respect of applications for extradition. Conversely, successive Governments in the Republic have been highly critical of security policies and practice in Northern Ireland and have reacted angrily to any incursion by the British Army or the RUC across the border.

These political disputes have not prevented the development of a good deal of practical co-operation in the exchange of information and in co-ordinated patrolling by the security forces on both sides. Any more far-reaching co-operation is likely to depend on the careful development of *reciprocal* cross-border arrangements. Unionists are keen to see more effective security co-operation in border areas but oppose the granting of any form of unilateral jurisdiction for the Republic in Northern Ireland. Nationalists on both sides of the border are equally sensitive about granting any right to British troops or even the RUC within the Republic. The only practicable approach is thus for both sides to agree on the *same* infringements of their cherished territorial sovereignty in the interests of more effective mutual security.

Extradition and Extra-Territorial Jurisdiction

The successful operation of reciprocal arrangements of this kind can be illustrated by the procedures for extra-territorial jurisdiction that were agreed after the Sunningdale conference in 1973 in default of agreement over extradition. The official position in the Republic, both in the courts and in government, was that it would be a breach of international law if anyone residing in the Republic who was suspected of or charged with terrorist offences in Northern Ireland or Britain were extradited, since his or her crimes were of a political nature. The view in Britain and Northern Ireland has long been that most terrorist offences would not qualify as political crimes and that in any event it is open to states to make special arrangements to deal with particular difficulties, as in the recent European Convention on the Suppression of Terrorism, which the Republic has as yet failed to sign.[4] Though recent decisions of the Supreme Court in the Republic, notably in the cases of *McGlinchy* and *Shannon*, have moved closer to the British position by refusing to treat the allegedly sectarian murder of civilians as political offences, it is as yet unclear whether this would extend to murders of members of the security forces. And there are other unresolved procedural problems over extradition, notably the requirement in most international extradition treaties – though not in the 'backing of warrants' procedure that currently applies between Britain and Northern Ireland and the Republic – that a prima facie case be established in the papers requesting extradition.[5]

The essence of the compromise agreed by the joint Law Enforcement Commission established at Sunningdale was that measures should be introduced to permit persons charged with any serious offence to be tried either in Northern Ireland or in the Republic wherever the offence was committed, and for evidence in respect of such cases to be heard in the other jurisdiction by the judge concerned if any witness refused to appear in the trial court. The provisions of the Criminal Jurisdiction Act 1975 in the United Kingdom and of the Criminal Law (Jurisdiction) Act 1976 in the Republic that gave effect to this compromise have not been frequently used. But they have been shown to be both workable and acceptable – as in one case in which a Northern Ireland judge heard evidence in Dublin in respect of a Diplock trial in Belfast.

A Cross-Border Security Zone

This reciprocal approach could readily be developed to deal with other problems. Neither extradition nor the procedures for extra-territorial jurisdiction make any provision for effective cross-border operations at earlier and, arguably, more crucial stages in the criminal process, notably the arrest and questioning of suspects and preventive action or surveillance.

One possibility would be the creation of a limited cross-border zone in which members of the security forces on either side could operate, with prior agreement, for the purposes of preventive surveillance and investigation. The precise extent of any such zone would clearly be a matter for negotiation but could perhaps be defined to cover all local authority districts contiguous to the border. Any such arrangements would, of course, be fully reciprocal, so that members of the security forces of the Republic would have the same rights in border areas of Northern Ireland as their counterparts in border areas of the Republic.

This suggestion has not been well-received either in Northern Ireland or in the Republic, not least because of the general resistance to the idea of granting the Irish or British Army any right of incursion across the border. Operations in a cross-border zone might therefore be restricted to the RUC and the Garda Siochána. This would avoid problems over the somewhat different basis of army operations on either side, in that the British Army has separate legal powers from the RUC and a measure of operational autonomy, while the Irish Defence Forces are restricted, both in law and in operational terms, to action in support of the Garda. It would also encourage the kind of co-operation between the two police forces discussed above. The most practicable model might be the development of a joint cross-border security unit along the lines of the regional crime squads that have been set up in Britain to deal with criminal activity that spans more than one police area. The role of the army on either side of the border would then be to act in support of such a joint police unit where necessary.

Reciprocal Judicial Arrangements

A further possibility in this context would be the extension of extra-territorial jurisdiction to cover not only the trial but also the prior police investigation of offences with a cross-border element. This would mean that where an offence had been committed in Northern Ireland and the suspect had been arrested in the Republic, he could opt for all aspects of the investigation to be dealt with by a joint RUC/Garda team. A similar procedure might be applied to all persons arrested under powers provided for a cross-border security zone. It would clearly be necessary for this purpose for both jurisdictions to adopt identical legislation to govern powers of arrest and questioning and other procedural matters in order to avoid any legal difficulties that might subsequently arise in bringing criminal proceedings to a successful conclusion. Since equivalent provisions have already been shown to be both constitutionally and politically acceptable in respect of the hearing of evidence, there should not be any major problems in this respect.

It would also be possible to provide for a judge or legal assessor from the other jurisdiction to sit in any case with a cross-border element, whether arising from the extradition of a suspect, the exercise of extra-territorial jurisdiction or the exercise of powers in a cross-border security zone. This might even be extended to provide for a judge from the other jurisdiction to sit as a member of the Special Criminal Court for terrorist offences in Dublin and of Diplock courts in Belfast. Since the purpose of any arrangement of this kind would be to increase public confidence in the decisions of the relevant court, it would be necessary to require any verdict to be unanimous. It would thus be possible to operate with a single judge from each jurisdiction. An additional advantage of this approach would be that it would not require the harmonization of criminal law and procedure in both jurisdictions and could therefore be implemented without any extended delay.

A Cross-Border Security Court

The final development of this reciprocal approach might be the establishment of a single cross-border court to deal with prescribed terrorist offences on either side of the border. There has been some interest in the Republic in this concept, not least as a means of boosting confidence among members of the minority community in Northern Ireland and among citizens of the Republic in the administration of justice in Northern Ireland. An all-Ireland court of this kind was viewed as a possibility by the joint Law Enforcement Commission in 1974 but was not pursued because of the pressure of time. It might be manned by judges from both jurisdictions, with or without an additional judge or observer from another European or common law jurisdiction. As in the case of a cross-border security zone, it would be necessary to establish identical rules of procedure for arrest and questioning and other pre-trial proceedings and to ensure that the substantive law on the relevant criminal offences was identical in order to avoid protracted and damaging procedural and constitutional wrangles. In formal legal terms this would not present insuperable difficulties, since the criminal law and the rules of criminal procedure are already broadly the same in both jurisdictions.[6] There would be likely to be substantial unionist resistance to such a programme, notwithstanding the fact that an all-Ireland court would have jurisdiction over cases that would otherwise have been the exclusive preserve of the courts in the Republic. It could be envisaged only within the context of a wider settlement of the kind outlined above, in which the Republic gave full recognition to the legitimacy of Northern Ireland. But the idea of a common court in which northern and southern judges would sit together, independently of both Governments, to deal with prescribed offences arising out of cross-border security operations, or more generally, would symbolize a new relationship between the two states in a particularly effective way.

Even if such a court were established, it would still be appropriate for the Republic to develop its approach to extradition, notably in respect of those accused of terrorist offences in Britain. The Irish Government should ratify the European Convention on the Suppression of Terrorism and alter its laws on extradition to distinguish between terrorist offences and other political offences. A reservation to the Convention might be made to reserve a discretion not to extradite in genuine cases of political persecution, as has been done by other European democracies.

If any of these proposals for cross-border security and judicial institutions were adopted as part of a wider settlement, there would be an obvious need for an inter-governmental security committee and for supervision and monitoring by an appropriate inter-state body. The form that this might take is best discussed in the broader context of a new relationship between Britain and Ireland.

9
Britain and Ireland: A New Relationship

The Northern Ireland issue has poisoned relationships between Britain and the Republic ever since 1920. Agreement on a comprehensive settlement that recognizes the respective rights and identities of the two communities in Northern Ireland would in itself create a new relationship between the two states. The need to take joint action over a period of years to implement the various parts of the package and to monitor the performance of the agencies involved would involve the creation of new joint institutions. But a new relationship need not be limited to that. There are many other shared concerns and interests that stem from the free movement of population between the two islands over the centuries, their shared social and cultural heritage and their high degree of economic interdependence. Similar historical and cultural links between the Nordic countries of Denmark, Sweden, Norway, Finland and Iceland have long been recognized in permanent political institutions centred on the Nordic Council, an inter-parliamentary body with representatives from each of the five countries.[1] A start was made on the process of creating equivalent links between Britain and Ireland by the establishment of a formal Anglo-Irish Inter-governmental Council after the Haughey/Thatcher summit in 1980. But the Council has no permanent existence apart from the periodic meetings between Ministers and civil servants. The development of permanent Anglo-Irish parliamentary and administrative institutions is long overdue.

Implementing and Monitoring a Settlement

The first step in implementing a settlement over Northern Ireland must be the ratification of a new Anglo-Irish treaty setting out the agreed status of Northern Ireland and a broad framework for future action to give full and equal recognition to the two communities there, as outlined in

101

Chapter 3. But that action is likely to be spread over a number of years, not least because it may not prove practicable to move with the same speed on all parts of the overall package – or even to agree initially on precisely what is to be done in all spheres. In that sense the treaty would not provide a detailed blueprint but would initiate and define a process.

This means that there is likely to be a need not only for a number of ad hoc commissions to study the practicalities of particular items but also for some more permanent mechanism to monitor progress and performance in each sphere. The joint Law Enforcement Commission established at the Sunningdale conference in 1973 may be taken as a useful model for the former. A similar body might well be established to work out the details of cross-border security arrangements outlined in Chapter 8. The task of monitoring progress and performance on a more permanent basis might be given to a joint parliamentary body composed of representatives of the Westminster Parliament and Oireachtas Éireann, the Parliament of the Republic, and perhaps also of any Northern Ireland assembly if agreement could be reached. A body of this kind, often referred to as a parliamentary tier to the Anglo-Irish Intergovernmental Council, has long been proposed, notably by the Kilbrandon Committee. But apart from the suggestion by Kilbrandon that it might act as a kind of legislature for Northern Ireland under a joint authority system of government, there has been little clear thinking on what such a parliamentary tier would actually do. As a result many have dismissed the proposal as likely to lead only to a talking shop. To give to the parliamentary tier the more precise function of monitoring progress within Northern Ireland on the various aspects of an overall settlement would resolve any initial problem in this respect. There are a number of matters that would initially be the shared responsibility of the two Governments in London and Dublin, notably the operation of any joint cross-border security arrangements. There are also a number of matters that would be the primary responsibility of the London Government, notably compliance with the terms of a Bill of individual and communal rights and the achievement of any prescribed targets in terms of equality of employment, but in which politicians in the Republic, as guarantors of the rights of northern Catholics, would have an obvious interest. On all such matters regular scrutiny by select specialist committees of an inter-parliamentary tier, with powers to call witnesses and require the production of papers, would help to ensure that the momentum of a settlement was maintained.

The relationship between a London–Dublin parliamentary tier and any arrangements for direct co-operation between Belfast and Dublin might cause some difficulty. The main unionist parties have indicated that they would not be prepared to participate in any body that would give any direct authority to representatives of the Republic over Northern Ireland. Even if this position were maintained in the face of a comprehensive settlement with guarantees for unionists and nationalists, it would not prevent representatives from Britain and the Republic from carrying on the work of a parliamentary tier. If, on the other hand, a devolved administration were eventually established in Belfast, it would be natural and desirable to give to any Northern Ireland assembly full responsibility for direct Belfast–Dublin relationships on all matters that had been devolved. This approach suggests that ultimately the role of the London–Dublin parliamentary tier should be limited to those matters that remain the primary responsibility of the London and Dublin Governments and that its membership should be limited to members of the London and Dublin Parliaments. Since the populations of Britain and the two parts of Ireland are so disproportionate, however, it would not be unreasonable to provide for a rough equality of membership from the Republic and from the United Kingdom as a whole, including a weighted representation of Northern Ireland MPs. It would then be for a future Northern Ireland assembly and the Irish Parliament to decide whether to create a separate or related parliamentary tier to scrutinize any direct Belfast–Dublin relationships. Since in practice institutions of this kind often develop in an untidy and irrational way, it would be better to ensure that the task of scrutiny was actually carried out than to insist on any particular formal or representative framework.

Permanent Institutions

The relationship between Britain and Ireland might be developed on a more permanent basis, both in respect of Northern Ireland and more generally. There is scope for a number of joint agencies to provide a more positive basis for co-operation on matters that have long been handled in a special way, such as the control of aliens and the substantial flow of workers and others between the two countries. Similar joint agencies might be established to handle matters of more recent concern. Special arrangements for the funding of agriculture in Northern Ireland within the Common Agricultural Policy have often proved necessary to limit the adverse effect of differing payments and tariffs north and south of the border and a formal joint agency for this purpose would almost certainly be welcomed by the European Commission. Similar arrangements might be made to co-ordinate the work of fisheries protection and other aspects of the exploitation of territorial waters. It would also be desirable to establish a jointly funded human rights commission with the tasks of promoting tolerance and combating religious and other prejudices through educational programmes and of monitoring performance on human rights issues. Joint bodies of this kind, with clear and explicit functions, would do more to cement the close relationships between the two countries than the somewhat nebulous role of Anglo-Irish Encounter, the only joint body that has to date been established, in promoting artistic and cultural exchanges.

All these bodies and agencies could appropriately be required to report to the Anglo-Irish Parliamentary Council. A permanent secretariat might also be created to administer monies provided for joint operations by the two Governments. The general objective would be to create an effective framework for the administration and supervision of functions and services that in practice call for a co-ordinated approach because of the established relationships between Britain and the two parts of Ireland rather than to set up apparently high-level structures for co-operation without any underlying foundation for joint action. While there is a high degree of community of interest between the two states, it would be unrealistic to ignore the fact that in other respects they have, and will continue to have, differing commitments and interests at both a political and an economic level.

Neutrality and Defence

One serious area of difference is likely to be neutrality and defence. Britain is a committed member of NATO and the Western bloc. Ireland since its formation has adhered strictly to a policy of neutrality and sees itself as an important link between the Western bloc and the Third World.[2] It has sometimes been suggested that this basic difference in approach, most recently highlighted by the refusal of the Republic to give any support to Britain over the Falklands war, might be resolved as part of a deal over Northern Ireland. For example, it has been argued that if Britain were to make a major concession to the Republic in respect of sovereignty over Northern Ireland, the Republic might agree to abandon its neutrality and join NATO. That is highly unrealistic. The commitment to neutrality in the Republic is almost certainly as deeply held as the aspiration to unification. Attempting to trade one for the other would be unacceptable to both North and South and would undermine any prospect of a general settlement.

The view that Britain clings tenaciously to its sovereignty over Northern Ireland only to retain its defence bases there is equally unconvincing. There are some important defence facilities in Northern Ireland, notably the advance-warning NATO installation at the Bishopscourt base in County Down. But the retention of these facilities is unlikely to be more than a marginal consideration in British policy on the Irish question. There are many precedents for the retention of military bases in the context of major political settlements, notably in respect of naval facilities in the so-called 'treaty ports' within the Republic retained by Britain under the Anglo-Irish Treaty of 1921, and of the air bases still retained in Cyprus. Some such arrangement could undoubtedly be negotiated if there were a serious intention on the part of the British to withdraw from Northern Ireland. The weakness of the similar argument that Britain insisted on maintaining its hold over Northern Ireland only to retain its economic investment there was conclusively demonstrated when most of the major British multinationals withdrew from the province in the mid-1970s. The essence of the Northern Ireland problem and the reason for the continuing British involvement in it are essentially political, not military or economic, however much some people on the left or the right may wish to believe otherwise.

10
Epilogue: Can it Really Work?

It is at this stage in the argument that the old questions emerge again. Yes, it may be said, all that is very interesting and probably true. But can it really work? Will a carefully balanced settlement that recognizes the legitimate claims of both communities please anyone? And if it will not, would it not be better in the long run to call the bluff of the unionists and move deliberately towards a united Ireland – or, alternatively, to ignore the northern nationalists, defeat the IRA and integrate Northern Ireland with the rest of Britain? To put the same point in more practical and immediate terms, could Mrs Thatcher and Dr Fitzgerald, if they were to adopt the kind of settlement outlined here, make it stick?

The answers to some of these questions have already been given. None of the straightforward solutions that ignore the identity and commitments of either of the two communities can be expected to work in present circumstances. It is not particularly helpful to suggest in response that they might work at some time in the future if circumstances were different. There is no reason to suppose that if nothing is done, or that if it is announced that a particular solution is to be adopted in the 1990s, circumstances will not change for the worse rather than improve in the intervening years. A more important question is whether a balanced cross-communal settlement can be made to work in the 1980s. The answer is that it can if there is sufficient determination to overcome the initial resistance that must be anticipated from all sides, if careful attention is paid to demonstrating the general acceptability of the package, and if there are sufficient economic incentives to induce the two communities in Northern Ireland to give it a try.

Facing Down the Opposition

There is certain to be a forceful reaction from politicians and paramilitaries on both sides to a serious attempt to implement a cross-communal settlement. On the unionist side it may be expected that the main political parties, the Official Unionists and the Democratic Unionists, will refuse to participate in a parliamentary tier with representatives from the Republic and that there will be threats of a renewed general strike similar to that which brought down the power-sharing Executive in 1974. On the republican side the immediate response is likely to be an increase in rioting and terrorist activity with a view to demonstrating the rejection of the package by committed nationalists and to antagonizing unionists and thus to making any compromise on their part more difficult. In the Republic it is likely that the Fianna Fáil opposition, led by Charles Haughey, will attempt to make political capital out of the failure of the governing coalition to adhere strictly to any of the three options in the New Ireland Forum Report.

The best response to challenges of this kind will be clear determination on the part of both Governments to press forward with those parts of the programme that do not require the active support of all parties in Northern Ireland and to resist any undemocratic challenge on the streets. Many of the measures that have been proposed, notably new arrangements for cross-border security and for greater reciprocity in the administration of justice, can be adopted by the London Government without the active support of the main Northern Ireland parties. Legislation can also be passed to devolve certain powers to a Northern Ireland assembly on a weighted majority basis as an inducement to those parties and individual members who are prepared to co-operate. It must also be made clear that the authorities will resist any attempt to mobilize support for a general strike by unlawful intimidation. The experience that has been gained by the RUC, the army and the Northern Ireland Office in dealing with threatened and actual stoppages of this kind since 1974 suggests that there is little to fear from this quarter in respect of any set of proposals that strikes a fair balance between the two communities.

In both these respects the record of Mrs Thatcher in persevering with her commitments will be of some significance. The position of the Government in the Republic is much less secure. Dr Fitzgerald's ability to deliver the Republic's side of the settlement and to resist any challenge from Charles Haughey either to the proposed settlement or to the coalition Government itself is likely to depend on clear evidence that the settlement is acceptable to northern Catholics as well as to a clear majority in the Republic. Within Northern Ireland the prospects of long-term stability for new arrangements will likewise be greatly increased if it can be shown conclusively that they are acceptable to a majority in both communities.

Establishing Acceptability

There is an important distinction between establishing the general acceptability of a settlement to both communities and establishing the level of
positive support for it. There is no solution to the Northern Ireland problem
that will gain the enthusiastic support of a majority in both communities.
It is sometimes even said in Northern Ireland that if a proposal is attacked
by both sides, then it must be right. That is clearly absurd. The converse
– that if a proposal is enthusiastically supported by one side, it is probably
wrong – is nearer to the mark. This means that a straightforward vote on
a particular package, whether in a separate referendum or in the context
of a general election for a Northern Ireland assembly or for the Westminster
Parliament, is unlikely to produce an accurate measure of acceptability.

This difficulty can be avoided if the co-operation of a sufficiently broad
spectrum of political parties can be secured to demonstrate broad acceptability. This was the strategy pursued during the Heath/Whitelaw settlement in 1973 prior to the creation of the power-sharing Executive. In
present circumstances it may be possible to secure the co-operation of the
Alliance Party and of at least a section of the SDLP. It is more doubtful
whether either of the two main unionist parties would be willing to offer
full co-operation, even as a means of obtaining a measure of devolution
to a Northern Ireland assembly under a weighted majority system. In these
circumstances the British Government may be forced to rely on a referendum in which the questions posed are carefully phrased so as to elicit some
measure of acceptability as well as of positive support. One possibility might
be to ask voters to choose between a proposed cross-communal settlement
and continuing direct rule on a first- and second-choice basis. This
approach was used to help resolve the impasse over the future of Newfoundland in the 1950s.[1] The power to put one or more issues to the
electorate in Northern Ireland that was provided under the Northern
Ireland Act 1974 (s. 2(3)) has now lapsed but could readily be renewed.

The situation in the Republic is rather different, since the major
contribution to the proposed settlement on the part of the Republic would
be a revision of Articles 2 and 3 of its Constitution, which currently assert
an ambiguous claim over Northern Ireland (see Chapter 3), and since
amendment to the Irish Constitution requires a referendum. The result of
such a referendum would be likely to depend largely on the stance of
constitutional nationalists in the North. Most of the population in the
Republic has a genuine attachment to the ideal of unification. Many would
welcome the opportunity to reflect such an idea in the Constitution and
would accept the implication that a united Ireland will have to be earned

and cannot be claimed as of right. Despite the likely opposition of the Fianna Fáil leadership to any settlement short of a unitary state, a majority in the Republic would probably support any settlement that appeared to satisfy John Hume and other leaders of constitutional nationalist opinion in the North.

Economic Inducements

Little has been said thus far about the problems of the economy of Northern Ireland and how it might be rescued from further decline. The major causes of the decline are common to other peripheral regions in Britain. Political instability in Northern Ireland has made only a marginal additional contribution. Although unemployment in Northern Ireland has always been about double that in Britain as a whole, it is still only a little worse than in Scotland and the North of England.[2] As in those regions, there is an urgent need for action to promote additional economic activity and investment. The more pertinent economic problem in this context, as has been shown, is the very substantial difference in employment levels and economic prosperity between the two communities.

The promise of greater economic prosperity if political stability could be achieved would none the less be a significant factor in increasing the general acceptability of a settlement. Greater economic prosperity would not in itself alter the loyalties and commitments of the two communities. As one witness put it vividly to the New Ireland Forum, northern Protestants would rather eat grass than agree to a united Ireland. But the prospect of more jobs would undoubtedly be a considerable inducement to the Catholic community if it were convinced that a fair share would go to Catholics. Similarly the assurance that, if a settlement were agreed, the promised increase in employment levels among Catholics would not have to be achieved at the expense of greater unemployment among Protestants would remove one of the major – though not always clearly articulated – fears of the unionist community. The repeated indications from the United States and from Europe that an agreed settlement of the Northern Ireland problem would lead to greatly increased levels of investment in Northern Ireland could thus play an important part in the process of securing agreement.

The serious economic problems in the Republic have equally not been emphasized. The heavy cost to a weak economy of security directly relating to the Northern Ireland conflict and the prospect of an even greater burden should no settlement be achieved will be significant factors in the response to any new arrangements there. Both the conservation of resources now spent on security and the greater external investment flowing from a settlement would be inducements as important to people in the Republic as to those in the North.

Success or Failure?

Whether these economic inducements and the determination of Mrs Thatcher and Dr Fitzgerald to make progress will be sufficient to break the shackles of traditional Irish nationalism and traditional unionism and allow a settlement to be reached in the current round of Anglo-Irish talks remains to be seen. In their communiqué following the Chequers summit in November 1984 the two premiers explicitly stated that they were seeking a settlement in which 'the identities of both the majority and the minority communities in Northern Ireland [would] be recognized and respected, and reflected in the structures and processes of Northern Ireland in ways acceptable to both communities' and in which 'the process of government in Northern Ireland [would] be such as to provide the people of both communities with the confidence that their rights will be safe-guarded'. The suggestions made in this book fall squarely within that framework.

The remaining area of disagreement appears to be the extent to which the Republic can be allowed to exercise direct authority over Northern Ireland. This is an important Irish objective, since it would allow Dr Fitzgerald to claim that the agreement was a development of the joint-authority option proposed by the New Ireland Forum. But Mrs Thatcher has repeatedly made it clear that she will not countenance any derogation from British sovereignty over Northern Ireland. The resolution of this difficulty suggested here is that any joint powers should be exercised on a reciprocal basis on both sides of the border. This too can be portrayed as a form of joint authority. But it is one that is consistent with the preservation of ultimate British sovereignty and with the full recognition by the Republic of the legitimacy of the current constitutional status of Northern Ireland.

Even if a general settlement along these lines cannot be reached this year, however, the realities and requirements identified here and in the Forum Report will remain. For more than a hundred years the Irish problem has defeated all those who have sought a solution based on the old concepts of nationalism and exclusive state sovereignty. If this book makes even a small contribution to the acceptance in London, Dublin and Belfast of a more complex but realistic framework, it will have served its purpose.

Appendix: The Realities and Requirements Identified in the New Ireland Forum Report
(paras. 5.1-5.3)

5.1   The major realities identified in the Forum's analysis of the problem, as set out in earlier chapters, may be summarized as follows: –

(1)   Existing structures and practices in Northern Ireland have failed to provide either peace, stability or reconciliation. The failure to recognize and accommodate the identity of Northern nationalists has resulted in deep and growing alienation on their part from the system of political authority.

(2)   The conflict of nationalist and unionist identities has been concentrated within the narrow ground of Northern Ireland. This has prevented constructive interaction between the two traditions and fostered fears, suspicions and misunderstandings.

(3)   One effect of the division of Ireland is that civil law and administration in the South are seen, particularly by unionists, as being unduly influenced by the majority ethos on issues which Protestants consider to be a matter for private conscience and there is a widespread perception that the South in its laws, attitudes and values does not reflect a regard for the ethos of Protestants. On the other hand, Protestant values are seen to be reflected in the laws and practices in the North.

(4)   The present formal position of the British Government, namely the guarantee, contained in Section 1 of the Northern Ireland Constitution Act, 1973, has in its practical application had the effect of inhibiting the dialogue necessary for political progress. It has had the additional effect of removing the incentive which would otherwise exist on all sides to seek a political solution.

(5)   The above factors have contributed to conflict and instability with disastrous consequences involving violence and loss of life on a large scale in Northern Ireland.

(6)   The absence of political consensus, together with the erosion of the North's economy and social fabric, threatens to make irreversible the drift into more widespread civil conflict with catastrophic consequences.

(7)   The resulting situation has inhibited and placed under strain the development of normal relations between Britain and Ireland.

(8)   The nationalist identity and ethos comprise a sense of national Irish identity and a democratically founded wish to have that identity institutionalized in a sovereign Ireland united by consent.

(9)   The unionist identity and ethos comprise a sense of Britishness, allied to their particular sense of Irishness and a set of values comprising a Protestant ethos which they believe to be under threat from a Catholic ethos, perceived as reflecting different and often opposing values.

(10)   Irish nationalist attitudes have hitherto in their public expression tended to underestimate the full dimension of the unionist identity and ethos. On the other hand, unionist attitudes and practices have denied the right of nationalists to meaningful political expression of their identity and ethos.

(11)   The basic approach of British policy has created negative consequences. It has shown a disregard of the identity and ethos of nationalists. In effect, it has underwritten the supremacy in Northern Ireland of the unionist identity. Before there can be fundamental progress Britain must reassess its position and responsibility.

5.2 Having considered these realities, the Forum proposes the following as necessary elements of a framework within which a new Ireland could emerge: –

(1)   A fundamental criterion of any new structures and processes must be that they will provide lasting peace and stability.

(2)   Attempts from any quarter to impose a particular solution through violence must be rejected along with the proponents of such methods. It must be recognized that the new Ireland which the Forum seeks can come about only through agreement and must have a democratic basis.

(3)   Agreement means that the political arrangements for a new and sovereign Ireland would have to be freely negotiated and agreed to by the people of the North and by the people of the South.

(4)   The validity of both the nationalist and unionist identities in Ireland and the democratic rights of every citizen on this island must be accepted; both of these identities must have equally satisfactory, secure and durable, political, administrative and symbolic expression and protection.

(5)   Lasting stability can be found only in the context of new structures in which no tradition will be allowed to dominate the other, in which there will be equal rights and opportunities for all, and in which there will be provision for formal and effective guarantees for the protection of individual human rights and of the communal and cultural rights of both nationalists and unionists.

(6) Civil and religious liberties and rights must be guaranteed and there can be no discrimination or preference in laws or administrative practices, on grounds of religious belief or affiliation; government and administration must be sensitive to minority beliefs and attitudes and seek consensus.

(7) New arrangements must provide structures and institutions including security structures with which both nationalists and unionists can identify on the basis of political consensus; such arrangements must overcome alienation in Northern Ireland and strengthen stability and security for all the people of Ireland.

(8) New arrangements must ensure the maintenance of economic and social standards and facilitate, where appropriate, integrated economic development, North and South. The macro-economic and financial implications are dealt with in the study by DKM Economic Consultants published with this Report, which is based on a range of assumptions with regard to the availability of external financial transfers.

(9) The cultural and linguistic diversity of the people of all traditions, North and South, must be preserved and fostered as a source of enrichment and vitality.

(10) Political action is urgently required to halt disillusionment with democratic politics and the slide towards further violence. Britain has a duty to respond *now* in order to ensure that the people of Northern Ireland are not condemned to yet another generation of violence and sterility. The parties in the Forum by their participation in its work have already committed themselves to join in a process directed towards that end.

5.3 It is clear that the building of a new Ireland will require the participation and co-operation of all the people of Ireland. In particular, it is evident that the people of the South must wholeheartedly commit themselves and the necessary resources to this objective. The parties in the Forum are ready to face up to this challenge and to accommodate the realities and meet the requirements identified by the Forum. However, Britain must help to create the conditions which will allow this process to begin. The British Government have a duty to join in developing the necessary process that will recognize these realities and give effect to these requirements and thus promote reconciliation between the two major traditions in Ireland, and to make the required investment of political will and resources. The British and Irish Governments should enter into discussions to create the framework and atmosphere necessary for this purpose.

Notes

Chapter 1
The Impasse: Why Everyone Despairs of the Irish Problem

1   These figures are taken from the New Ireland Forum study, *The Cost of Violence Arising from the Northern Ireland Crisis since 1969* (Dublin: Stationery Office, 1983).

2   The figures for road deaths are taken from the annual reports of the RUC Traffic Branch and *Traffic Statistics: Great Britain 1973–1983*, which includes international comparisons in Table 6.9 (London: HMSO, 1984); the murder rates are taken from the Policy Planning Unit, Occasional Paper No. 5, *A Commentary on Northern Ireland Crime Statistics 1969–1982* (Belfast: Department of Finance and Personnel, 1984). The figures for Northern Ireland include the small number of non-terrorist murders. For a more detailed, though dated, analysis see D. R. Bates, 'If You Think Belfast is Dangerous ...', *Fortnight: An Independent Review for Northern Ireland*, issue 91, October 1974, which shows that the ordinary murder rate in many large American cities in 1970 was higher than the worst Northern Ireland figures of 1972.

Chapter 2
The Simple Solutions: Why They will not Work

1   A (very) short list might include, on the historical background, A. T. Q. Stewart, *The Narrow Ground: Aspects of Ulster 1609–1969* (London: Faber & Faber, 1977) and D. W. Miller, *Queen's Rebels* (Dublin: Gill & Macmillan, 1978); on the Stormont regime, R. Rose, *Governing Without Consensus* (London: Faber & Faber, 1971) and M. Farrell, *Northern Ireland: The Orange State* (London: Pluto Press, 1976); on the social and economic background, J. Darby (ed.), *Northern Ireland: The Background to the Conflict* (Belfast: Appletree Press, 1983); and on the current situation, P. O'Malley, *The Uncivil War* (Belfast: Blackstaff Press, 1984).

2   The argument about whether Ireland is or is not a natural political unit is discussed in J. Bowman, *De Valera and the Northern Question 1917–1973* (Oxford: Clarendon Press, 1982).

3   The Report of the New Ireland Forum is published by the Stationery Office, Dublin. The Forum also published a series of important research studies: *The Macroeconomic Consequences of Integrated Economic Policy, Planning and Co-ordination in Ireland*; *The Economic Consequences of the Division of Ireland since 1920*; *A Comparative Description of the Economic Structure and Situation North and South*; *The Cost of Violence Arising from the Northern Ireland Crisis since 1969*; *The Legal Systems North and South*; and *An Analysis of Agricultural Developments in the North and South of Ireland and of the Effects of Integrated Policy and Planning*. All of these may also be obtained from the Stationery Office.

4   *Report of the Irish Boundary Commission 1925*, with an introduction by G. J. Hand (Shannon: Irish University Press, 1969).

5   *Fortnight: An Independent Review for Northern Ireland*, issue 192, March 1983; see also P. Compton, 'The Demographic Background' in D. Watt (ed.), *The Constitution of Northern Ireland: Problems and Prospects* (London: Heinemann, 1981). Figures for the strength of the two communities cannot be precise, since in the official censuses of 1971 and 1981 the question on religion was not compulsory. In 1981 19 per cent of householders refused to answer it, and there was also a partial boycott of the whole census in some republican areas.

6   In evidence to the Forum Frank Curran estimated that the Catholic population was between 620,000 and 640,000, representing 40 per cent of the total population of Northern Ireland, and that in the three western counties Catholics were in a two-to-one majority (*Minutes of Evidence No. 6*, p. 25ff.).

7   *The Macroeconomic Consequences of Integrated Economic Policy, Planning and Co-ordination in Ireland*, Davy Kelleher & McCarthy Ltd, p. 21; in 1983 the British subvention amounted to about 30 per cent of gross national product in Northern Ireland, and its replacement by a direct transfer from the Republic would amount to 12 per cent of gross national product in the Republic.

8   Ibid., p. 16; on this basis the contribution from the Republic to a total subvention of some IR£1,600 million would in 1983 have been about IR£60 million (3.7 per cent), a figure that would not impose a substantial burden on the Republic's economy (see ch. 6).

9   The case for an independent Northern Ireland was argued in *Beyond the Religious Divide*, a pamphlet published by the New Ulster Political Research Group in 1978; in it John Simpson, a senior lecturer in economics at

Queen's University, Belfast, and Senator T. K. Whitaker, a former Governor of the Central Bank of Ireland, both took the view that on favourable assumptions an independent Northern Ireland would be economically viable. The economic consultants to the Forum, Davy Kelleher & McCarthy, though they were not asked to give a direct view on the issue, concluded that an economically independent Northern Ireland within a federal Ireland would be financially unviable without any British subvention and that even with substantial British and European aid unemployment would rise substantially in the 1990s (see *Macroeconomic Consequences of Integrated Economic Policy, Planning and Co-ordination in Ireland*, ch. 5). For a more general view of the independence option see Dervla Murphy, *Changing the problem: Post-Forum Reflections* (Mullingar: Lilliput Press, 1984).

10   *Report of the Irish Boundary Commission 1925*, with an introduction by G. J. Hand (Shannon: Irish University Press, 1969); the Irish representative, Eóin MacNeill, agreed to the Commission's draft recommendations but then resigned when they were leaked to the *Morning Post*.

11   P. Compton, 'The Demographic Background' (see above).

12   A unilateral British withdrawal means the withdrawal of British troops and British administration and not the enforced expulsion of the Protestant community. The republican slogan 'Brits Out' is ambiguous on this point.

13   On these issues see M. McDougal, H. D. Laswell and Lung-Chu Chen, *Human Rights and World Public Order: The Basic Policies of an International Law of Human Dignity* (New Haven: Yale University Press, 1980), and J. Dugard, *The Denationalisation of Black South Africans in Pursuance of Apartheid* (Lawyers for Human Rights, 1984).

Chapter 3

A New Framework: Reflecting the Realities

1   The extent of existing and possible future co-operation on rights of citizenship, economic co-operation and mutual understanding was reviewed by a series of Anglo-Irish working parties in 1981, *Anglo-Irish Joint Studies* (Dublin: Government Information Services, Pl. 299, 1981).

2   The interpretation of Articles 2 and 3 is discussed in detail in *The Legal Systems, North and South*, a study prepared for the New Ireland Forum by Professor Boyle and Professor Greer (Dublin: Stationery Office, 1984), pp. 17–20.

3   (1974) IR 338.

4   On a strict interpretation the guarantee rules out only the total exclusion of Northern Ireland from the United Kingdom or any form of repartition

– a point not widely recognized – but not other constitutional changes; and in any event there is nothing in British law to prevent the simple repeal of the whole guarantee.

5   There was provision in the Anglo-Irish Treaty of 1921 for both Northern and Southern Ireland to provide safeguards for their respective minorities if Northern Ireland had agreed to remain in the Irish Free State; there was no equivalent provision if, as both parties accepted was inevitable, Northern Ireland opted out.

6   Government of Ireland Act 1920, s. 8 (in respect of Northern Ireland) and Art. 5.5 of the Irish Constitution (in respect of the Republic); see generally H. Calvert, *Constitutional Law in Northern Ireland* (Belfast: Northern Ireland Legal Quarterly, 1968), and C. Palley, 'The Evolution, Disintegration, and Possible Reconstruction of the Northern Ireland Constitution', *Anglo-American Law Review* (1973), pp. 368–476, and R. Fanning, *Independent Ireland* (Dublin: Helicon Press, 1983), ch. 1.

7   See C. A. Macartney, 'League of Nations Protection of Minority Rights', in E. Luard (ed.), *The International Protection of Human Rights* (New York: Praeger, 1967).

8   Cmnd 8541.

Chapter 4
Northern Ireland: Why it Failed

1   The best-known account of communal separation in a rural setting is in R. Harris, *Prejudice and Tolerance in Ulster* (Manchester: Manchester University Press, 1972); for an account of an urban community during the 'troubles' see F. Burton, *The Politics of Legitimacy: Struggles in a Belfast Community* (London: Routledge & Kegan Paul, 1978).

2   See Fair Employment Agency, *An Industrial and Occupational Profile of the Two Sections of the Population in Northern Ireland* (Belfast, 1978).

3   For a general account of security policies and practices in this period see M. Farrell, *Arming the Protestants: The Formation of the Ulster Special Constabulary and the Royal Ulster Constabulary 1920–1927* (Dingle: Brandon, 1984).

4   P. Buckland, *A History of Northern Ireland* (Dublin: Gill and Macmillan, 1981), p. 46.

5   For an official account of these and other discriminatory practices see the report of the Cameron Commission, *Disturbances in Northern Ireland*, Cmd 532 (Belfast: HMSO, 1969).

6   The provision under section 14 of the Government of Ireland Act 1920
     for elections to the Stormont Parliament to be by proportional representa-
     tion was repealed by the House of Commons (Method of Voting and
     Redistribution of Seats) Act (Northern Ireland) 1929; the corresponding
     provision in respect of local government elections had been repealed under
     the Local Government Act (Northern Ireland) 1922 with effect from 1923.

7   Fair Employment Agency, *An Industrial and Occupational Profile of the Two
     Sections of the Population in Northern Ireland* (see above).

8   R. Cathcart, *The Most Contrary Region: The BBC in Northern Ireland 1924–
     1984* (Belfast: Blackstaff Press, 1984).

9   See generally J. Bowman, *De Valera and the Northern Question 1917–
     1973* (Oxford: Clarendon Press, 1982).

10   See generally B. M. Walsh, *Religion and Demographic Behaviour in Ireland*
     (Dublin: Economic and Social Research Institute, 1970); on the role of
     the Catholic Church see J. Whyte, *Church and State in Modern Ireland*
     (Dublin: Gill & Macmillan, 1980), and R. Fanning, *Independent Ireland*
     (Dublin: Helicon Press, 1983).

Chapter 5
Direct Rule: Why it has not Helped

1   K. Boyle, T. Hadden and P. Hillyard, *Ten Years On in Northern Ireland: The
     Legal Control of Political Violence* (London: Cobden Trust, 1980).

2   Cmnd 5185 (1972).

3   F. Kitson, *Low Intensity Operations: Subversion, Insurgency and Peacekeeping*
     (London: Faber & Faber, 1971); many of the strategies pursued by the
     British Army in its early years in Northern Ireland may be linked with
     this book.

4   Cmnd 5847 (1975).

5   Cmnd 7497 (1979).

6   P. Taylor, *Beating the Terrorists?* (Harmondsworth: Penguin, 1980).

7   New Ireland Forum, *The Cost of Violence Arising from the Northern Ireland
     Crisis since 1969* (Dublin: Stationery Office, 1983), p. 7.

8   For a full account see R. Fisk, *The Point of No Return: The Strike which
     Broke the British in Ulster* (London: André Deutsch, 1975).

9   A useful summary of the legislation is given in the report of the standing
     Advisory Commission on Human Rights, *The Protection of Human Rights*

by Law in Northern Ireland, Cmnd 7009 (London: HMSO, 1977), ch. 2.

10   These figures are taken from the official reports of the 1981 census; see especially the report on *Religion* (Belfast: HMSO, 1984), Table 8; the unemployment rate for those who refused to give their religion was 24 per cent for men and 15 per cent for women, and for those who declared themselves as Protestants or as members of other non-Catholic religions the rate was 12 per cent for men and 9 per cent for women.

11   The work of the Agency both on individual complaints and on more general investigations of patterns of employment is summarized in its annual reports; for the recent investigations into the Northern Ireland Civil Service and the Fire Authority for Northern Ireland, both of which revealed compelling evidence of past if not current discrimination, see the *Eighth Report for 1983–84* (London: HMSO, 1985).

12   R. D. Osborne and R. Murray, *Educational Qualifications and Religious Affiliation in Northern Ireland*, Research Paper 3 (Belfast: Fair Employment Agency, 1978), and R. D. Osborne, *Religion and Educational Qualifications in Northern Ireland*, Research Paper 8 (Belfast: Fair Employment Agency, 1985).

Chapter 6
The Internal Dimension: New Structures Within Northern Ireland

1   The need for this recognition was accepted in general terms by the Official Unionist Party in *Devolution and the Northern Ireland Assembly: The Way Forward* (Belfast, 1984); some of the measures needed in the area of joint citizenship are discussed in the *Reports of the Anglo-Irish Joint Studies* (Dublin: Government Information Services, 1981).

2   *Belgian Linguistics case* (1965).

3   For a useful discussion of many of these issues see J. Fawcett, *The International Protection of Minorities*, Report No. 41 (London: Minority Rights Group, 1979).

Chapter 7
The Role of the Republic

1   *Report of the Committee on the Constitution* Prl. 9817 (Dublin: Stationery Office, 1967); the suggested rewording for Article 3 was: '1. The Irish nation hereby proclaims its firm will that its territory be re-united in harmony and brotherly affection between all Irishmen. 2. The laws enacted by the Parliament established by this Constitution shall, until the achieve-

ment of the nation's unity shall otherwise require, have the like area and extent of application as the Laws of the Parliament which existed prior to the adoption of this Constitution. Provision may be made by law to give extra-territorial effect to such laws.' No mention was made of the claim in Article 2 that the national territory should extend over the whole island of Ireland.

2   See the report of the *Joint Study on Economic Co-operation* (Dublin: Government Information Services, 1981).

3   *Higher Education in Ireland: Co-operation and Complementarity* (Williams Report) (Belfast and Dublin: Northern Ireland Economic Council and National Economic and Social Council, 1985).

Chapter 8
Security: Defending a Settlement

1   The contribution of the New Ireland Forum to security was limited to a detailed study of the incidence of violence and the cost to Britain and the Republic of dealing with it – *The Cost of Violence Arising from the Northern Ireland Crisis since 1969* (Dublin: Stationery Office, 1983) – and to a reiteration of the responsibility of the British Government for dealing with abuses and of the urgent need for a political settlement (paras. 4.1–4.5).

2   Public Order (Northern Ireland) Order 1981, Arts. 3(1) and 4(2), re-enacting Public Order Act (Northern Ireland) 1950, s. 1, and Public Order (Amendment) Act (Northern Ireland) 1970, s. 2.

3   Cmnd 9222 (London: HMSO, 1984); see also, for example, *Report of the Commission to consider legal procedures to deal with terrorist activities in Northern Ireland* (Diplock Report), Cmnd 5185 (London: HMSO, 1972), and *Report of the Tribunal appointed to inquire into events on Sunday, 30th January 1972, which led to loss of life in connection with the procession in Londonderry on that day* (Widgery Report), HC 220 (London: HMSO, 1972).

4   The views of the Republic and Britain are exhaustively stated in the *Report of the Law Enforcement Commission*, Cmnd 5627 (London: HMSO, 1974) and Prl. 3832 (Dublin: Stationery Office, 1974), chs. 6 and 7.

5   Ibid., ch. 3; the relevant statutes are, for the United Kingdom, the Backing of Warrants (Republic of Ireland) Act 1965 and, for the Republic, the Extradition Act 1965, Part III; for a general review see the recent discussion in *Extradition*, Cmnd 9421 (London: HMSO, 1985).

6   C. K. Boyle and D. S. Greer, *The Legal Systems, North and South: A Study Prepared for the New Ireland Forum* (Dublin: Stationery Office, 1984).

Chapter 9
Britain and Ireland: A New Relationship

1   The Nordic Council, established in 1953, has a permanent secretariat and, since 1971, a Council of Ministers with limited powers to act on a unanimous basis. The major areas of co-operation have been in respect of a common labour market, the harmonization of laws in certain spheres, regional trade and industrial development, and cultural affairs. For a recent account see G. P. Nielsson, 'The Parallel National Action Process: Scandinavian Experiences' in P. Taylor and A. J. R. Groom (eds.), *International Organisation: A Conceptual Approach* (London: Frances Pinter, 1978).

2   P. Keatinge, *A Singular Stance: Irish Neutrality in the 1980s* (Dublin: Institute of Public Administration, 1984).

Chapter 10
Epilogue: Can it Really Work?

1   *Documents on Relations between Canada and Newfoundland*, Volume 2, 1940–1949, Part I (Ottawa: Department of External Affairs, 1984); see also *Discussion Paper 2: Constitutional Convention Procedure* (London: HMSO, 1974), Annex B.

2   John Simpson, 'Economic Development: Cause and Effect in the Northern Ireland Conflict', in J. Darby (ed.), *Northern Ireland: The Background to the Conflict* (Belfast: Appletree Press, 1983), Table 4.1; in the 1950s and 1960s the position was relatively worse, with unemployment levels three or four times that in England.

Index

125

Index